LOVE AND CHANCE

When schoolteacher Megan bumps into a gorgeous Frenchman in the Hall of Mirrors at Versailles, she thinks she will never see him again. Until the Headteacher asks her to visit Lulu Santerre, a pupil who is threatening not to return to school. Megan discovers that Lulu's brother Raphael is the man she met at Versailles ... When Lulu goes missing Raphael and Megan are thrown together and both of them have to make decisions about their future.

Books by Susan Sarapuk
in the Linford Romance Library:

COMING HOME
WITHIN THESE WALLS

SUSAN SARAPUK

LOVE AND CHANCE

Complete and Unabridged

LINFORD
Leicester

First published in Great Britain in 2011

First Linford Edition
published 2012

British Library CIP Data

Sarapuk, Susan.
   Love and chance. - -
   (Linford romance library)
   1. Love stories.
   2. Large type books.
   I. Title II. Series
   823.9'2–dc23

   ISBN 978–1–4448–1037–0

Published by
F. A. Thorpe (Publishing)
Anstey, Leicestershire

Set by Words & Graphics Ltd.
Anstey, Leicestershire
Printed and bound in Great Britain by
T. J. International Ltd., Padstow, Cornwall
This book is printed on acid-free paper

1

How like her sister to have a tasteful apartment in the chic Marais area of Paris, Megan Honeyman thought, all white walls, mellow wooden floors, high ceilings and panoramic windows. Megan felt like a poor relation as she stood in the hallway with her case and a bag slung over her cagouled shoulder. Sarah, clothed in a cream linen dress with discreet pearls at her throat, looked every inch the executive's wife.

'So you found us,' she greeted her.

Megan nodded. 'This is beautiful,' she said, letting her gaze follow the architraving of the ceiling, appreciating the elegant proportions of the eighteenth century architechture.

Sarah smiled, pleased. 'We think so. Why don't you dump your stuff and come into the kitchen? I'll make us some coffee.'

1

Shrugging off her cagoule Megan followed her sister into the kitchen, its stainless steel surfaces seeming a little incongruous in the old building. She sat on a stool at the island as Sarah began to percolate coffee.

'How has school been this year?' her sister asked.

'The usual ups and downs.'

'You've been there eighteen months now. I thought it was just meant to fill a gap.'

'I like it. It suits me for now.'

Sarah frowned at her as she set out two dainty cups.

'You'd better be careful that you don't end up another Miss Jean Brodie,' she warned.

Megan sighed. 'For your information, Mike Havers, the Science master is interested.'

'You've mentioned him before. Didn't you say he wasn't your type?'

Megan shrugged. Sarah was right, but choice was limited in a girls' boarding school in the middle of nowhere.

'Well, I'm here for the summer,' she said. 'Maybe I'll fall in love.'

'Everyone leaves Paris in August. It'll be full of tourists,' Sarah said.

'Then at least we'll have a chance to get together,' said Megan. It was just the two of them now, since their parents' tragic accident three years before.

Sarah gave a cool smile. Megan knew she would relish the opportunity to show how much better she was doing than her elder sister — high-flying business-man husband, chic Paris apartment, a job at a prestigious art gallery. Megan didn't mind, but sensed that that riled Sarah who'd always been competitive. Sarah poured coffee. 'Cream?'

'I take it black.'

'Oh yes, I forgot.'

The coffee tasted bitter.

'So what are your plans for the summer?' Sarah asked.

'I'm going to search out baroque Paris,' Megan helped herself to a lump of sugar. 'Complete my research on

Louis XIV, maybe make a start on the book I've been threatening to write.'

'You know I'll be working?'

'Don't worry about me; I can amuse myself.' After being cooped up in school for so long she was looking forward to some time alone.

'We eat at eight most evenings,' Sarah informed her.

'What time will Tom be home?'

'He might have to work late,' Sarah said uncertainly. 'They're really busy at the moment. Would you like to see your room?'

The bedroom was as tasteful as the rest of the apartment with two classic French armoires and a sleigh bed.

'Make yourself at home,' Sarah invited her. 'Will you excuse me? I need to make some phone calls.'

Megan began to unpack, not that she'd brought much — mostly flimsy tops and skirts in anticipation of a hot Parisian summer. As she put them away in vanilla scented drawers, she suddenly thought of Dev and of all the hot places they'd planned to visit, She shook herself.

That was two years ago! Two years ago to the day in fact. She'd been trying to push it out of her mind all day. That day when Dev had told her that he wasn't going to travel the world with her after all, that he'd been offered a job in New York by Cara's father. It was then she discovered that he'd been seeing Cara behind her back.

Well, she'd managed to make something of herself since then, sort of. With a sigh she placed her canvas espadrilles on the shoe rack. She'd only been half joking when she'd said she'd come to Paris to fall in love — she certainly hadn't managed it at home, although the jury was still out on Mike Havers.

★ ★ ★

There was no sign of Sarah when Megan emerged from the bedroom. Someone was in the kitchen though, a short, middle-aged woman with her hair pinned in a neat chignon. She was wearing a chef's apron and chopping up vegetables.

'Bonjour,' Megan ventured.

'Bonjour, Madame,' said the woman. 'You are Megan?'

'That's right.'

'I am Madame Boursin, the cook.'

'Ah, yes. Pleased to meet you.' Megan picked up a cherry tomato from a bowl and savoured it. The click of the door made her turn.

'I'm home!' came a familiar voice and then her brother-in-law appeared in the kitchen doorway. 'Megan, you're here.' He greeted her with a hug. He'd always been tactile, a big bear of an American. 'Good to see you. How are you?' He went to the fridge, poured himself a glass of iced water and gulped it down. 'How was the train? The last time I went to London we were stuck in that tunnel for two hours!'

'The train was fine,' she laughed. 'But I'm always glad to get through the tunnel. I get a bit claustrophobic.'

Sarah reappeared.

'Oh you didn't have to work late after all!' She sounded surprised.

'I knew Megan was coming. It would have been rude not to be here,' Tom kissed his wife chastely on the cheek. Megan detected a hint of coolness in her sister's response.

'Let me dress for dinner,' Sarah said.

Megan didn't see the point of changing; she was happy in her jeans.

Tom winked at her affably. 'Just going to shower away the grime of the day,' he said, leaving her alone with Madame Boursin. The cook shook her head, clicked her tongue, and started muttering to herself in French. Megan had the impression that all was not well in paradise.

★ ★ ★

'So, Megs, how have you been? How's school?' Tom asked as the three of them sat down at one end of a table big enough to seat fourteen.

'School's good. I'm an assistant house mistress now.'

'Quick promotion.'

'Extra work.' She grimaced.

'How's the pay?' Sarah interjected.

'Put it this way, I don't live the high life but I'm not poor either.'

'Best way to be,' Tom agreed.

Sarah rolled her eyes. 'Darling, I don't think you'd want to be without this,' she looked round at the opulent surroundings.

'Hey, I love my job, but it's not about the money, it's about the challenge. And, Megs, it's gotta be cool shaping young minds.'

'Keeping them out of mischief more like.' Megan laughed.

'What's your subject, History?'

'With a bit of English thrown in. And sometimes I'm commandeered to coach tennis. You just learn to muck in at a boarding school.'

'I don't think I could cope with kids twenty-four hours a day,' Sarah pushed her plate aside and dabbed daintily at her mouth with a napkin.

'Kids would be great,' Tom enthused.

'Noisy, demanding things,' Sarah countered.

For a moment something hung in the air between them.

'Well I'm just glad to be away from them for the summer,' Megan said lightly. 'This is me-time. Thanks for allowing me to stay.'

'It's our pleasure, Megs,' Tom beamed.

She got the uncomfortable feeling that he was happy to have someone else besides his wife around.

'What's your plan for your first day in Paris?' he asked.

'I think I'll take a trip out to Versailles,' she said. 'It's years since I've been there.'

'I've never been,' he said.

'And you an American?' She punched him playfully on the arm. 'What about your reputation for being avid tourists?'

'Life's too busy to visit stately homes,' Sarah said tartly.

But you could always make time for

the things you wanted to do, Megan mused. What a shame to live in Paris yet never really explore it.

After dinner Tom disappeared into the study to work.

'Are things all right with you two?' She broached the subject with her sister as they sipped glasses of wine.

'Fine,' Sarah answered rather tersely. 'Tom's working hard, he's hoping for promotion.'

'I get the feeling he'd like to start a family.'

'Yes, well, what he'd like and what's going to happen are two different things. I've got my career to consider.' Sarah rose abruptly. 'Are you all right on your own? I need a bath and an early night. I've got an important client coming in tomorrow morning.'

'Fine,' Megan said. She might have wanted to catch up with her sister they'd not seen each other for so long; there were things they needed to talk about, the accident in particular. But Sarah was clearly not in the mood this evening and she had the whole of the holiday to bring up the subject of their parents.

'I'll be gone early in the morning,' Sarah paused in the doorway. 'You'll need to take the RER to Versailles.'

'I think I can manage,' Megan smiled. 'I have travelled before.'

She was looking forward to adventure in the city of romance.

2

When Megan got up the following morning both Sarah and Tom had indeed gone. She showered and dressed and then sauntered into the kitchen to find Madame Boursin there.

'Croissants, Madame? Coffee?' the older woman offered.

'Do you live in, Madame Boursin?' Megan asked as she watched the cook lay a tray for her.

'Non. I come mornings, five days. Late afternoon four days. I live in Porte de Saint-Ouen.'

She must start very early then, Megan reasoned.

'How long have you worked for my sister?'

'Eight months. Before them Monsieur Drieux lived here. Ah, what a gentleman.' Suddenly aware of the possible unfavourable comparison with her current employers, Madame Boursin stopped speaking and poured Megan's coffee.

Megan took the tray into the morning-room. French windows opened onto a small balcony above a communal garden. The early morning sun was already warm. She munched her croissant, watching swallows duck and dive under the eaves of the apartment building across the way.

Megan always savoured that luxurious feeling at the beginning of the school holidays — no breakfasts in the refectory with the constant buzz of student conversation, no mentally gearing up for the day ahead. Freedom! And real French croissants and coffee!

The whole summer stretched before her. It was time to begin the task she'd been putting off for so long — the book she'd always wanted to write about Louis XIV. Dev had often teased her about her passion: 'You just like men in ribbons and frilly shirts.'

'No,' she'd answered patiently. 'I like

men who know their own minds, men who can handle power and don't need to prove anything.'

Maybe that's why he'd gone, because he knew he'd never measure up. But it had never been her intention to judge him against heroes from history. Anyway, he was history now. She had no regrets.

After breakfast Megan packed her bag and set off, the ornate front door dispatching her immediately onto the street.

Paris smelled different from home — it was redolent of the peatiness of the river, caffeine and cigarette smoke from pavement cafes. Car horns beeped and motorcyclists weaved in and out of the traffic. Crossing busy roads was a lesson in the art of survival.

Megan's GCSE French got her a ticket on the RER out to Versailles. As she strolled down the main street, the palace in all its splendour rose up through ornamental gates and railings. Garish coaches disgorged hordes of tourists with their cameras and back-packs.

She tried to visualise the scene as it must have looked when the chateau was new, imagining the ambassadors drawing up in their carriages gasping at the glory of France, and the courtiers battling to find room to live and catch the eye of the Sun King. And now the masses were overrunning the place that had been meant for the nobility, she thought wryly as she queued up to pay her entrance fee.

If only she could have had the place to herself! Instead she was forced to squeeze through crowds gathered around tour guides as she tried to make her way through the state apartments. In the Hall of Mirrors she saw myriad reflections of strangers. Looking out through the grand windows, she saw tourists swarming over the gardens like ants.

When the crowds became too much Megan wandered in the grounds finally finding some seclusion as she walked through the woods towards the Petit and Grand Trianons. Here at least she could imagine herself back in the seventeenth century, believe that the Sun King himself might appear around the corner of a hedge accompanied by his courtiers.

Eventually she found a place to sit under the shade of some trees where she could look back towards the palace and pulled out her notebook. All the research had been done. Now it was a case of soaking herself in the atmosphere of the places where the events she'd read about had taken place.

Maybe Dev had been right, she smiled to herself. She did like ribbons and lace and frilly shirts. Why didn't men make an effort these days? In school the teachers all had to wear academic gowns on Founder's Day; and that was when she'd first considered whether she could fall for Mike the Science master. He'd looked quite dashing in his black gown.

He'd wanted them to meet up over

the holiday. She'd told him she'd be staying in Paris with her sister for the whole of the summer.

'Maybe I'll come to Paris for a few days,' he'd said.

'I'm not sure what plans my sister's made.'

'Why don't I ring you in a couple of weeks?' Mike hadn't been dissuaded. 'You'll know the lie of the land by then.'

So that had been the agreement. Megan wondered now whether she would welcome the phone call, for he was part of her school life and she didn't want to think of school during her vacation.

She looked up as a canoodling young couple passed by. When they decided to sit on the grass not far from her she closed her pad and got up to leave. This was authenticity, she told herself, French-speaking lovers; this is what it would have been like with the Versailles courtiers. Still, she didn't want to face it today.

Megan made her way back towards

the palace. The numbers were thinning as the afternoon drew on. She made a mental note that when she came back again it would be either very early in the morning or at the end of the day. Thinking she might have time to take one last look at the Hall of Mirrors, Megan hurried back inside the palace. People were beginning to disperse through the state rooms as the ushers tried to clear the building. She ducked down, attempting to sneak behind the line of tourists.

There were still some stragglers in the grand room, which felt close from the warmth of the day and the procession of countless bodies. Megan looked around, trying to take in all the details, scribbling notes in her pad as she went along.

'Non, Madame.' Suddenly an officious-looking person hurried towards her. 'Le Chateau est fermé maintenant. Is closed.'

'Yes, all right, I'm just leaving.' She turned with a sigh, fumbling to replace her notebook in her bag, and walked straight into someone who was entering the room.

'Pardonnez-moi, Madame.'

'No, I'm sorry. I should look where I'm going.' Megan looked up.

Standing before her was a man dressed in a dinner suit. His dark, almost black hair was neatly styled and brushed the collar of his pristine white shirt. His olive skin was clean-shaven. Brown eyes looked concerned as he extended a hand to steady her.

'Are you all right?' He switched to English.

'It was my fault,' Megan protested, flustered. The air around the stranger was filled with a delicious scent of coconut and vanilla and a darker spice she couldn't identify.

The official began to speak to the man in a flood of French, too fast for Megan to follow. From the tone, she guessed it was along the lines of 'tiresome tourists, no regard for rules, always thinking that they deserve one last look around.' The man shrugged and said something in reply.

'I'm leaving,' Megan said, hating to be thought of as a tourist. She hesitated in the doorway, unable to resist looking back. Her stomach did a flip. Now why couldn't men like him turn up at school? Mike Havers seemed insipid in comparison.

Megan hurried out of the building. She could feel her cheeks were flushed. As she made her way across the courtyard she saw a group of people in tuxedos and evening dress arriving through the gilded gates. There was obviously some sort of function at the palace tonight.

Nothing quite so glamorous for her. She retraced her steps to the station and caught the train back into the city.

'Did you have a good day?' Sarah asked later, back at the apartment.

'Great. I literally bumped into this gorgeous man in a tux as I was leaving Versailles. Why are French men so attractive?'

'Americans are pretty fine, too,' Sarah said.

'I'm obviously living in the wrong country.' Megan sighed. 'How about you, good day at work?'

'I sold thirty-thousand euros worth of paintings today.'

'Wow!'

Her sister shrugged. 'You know, Megan, you could be doing an exciting job if you put your mind to it.'

'But I don't want to,' Megan answered, wondering if her sister was going to be on her back for the duration of her stay.

'So you're going to stay in school forever?'

'No.'

'Well, it's your life.' Sarah sighed. 'I've got to change.'

Megan watched her leave. Sarah was slim, too skinny really, in her simple black dress and high heels. Would she want to be like her? She didn't think so. She smiled to herself now as she thought of the handsome Frenchman in

21

the dinner suit. It was only her first day and she'd already come across the most gorgeous man she'd seen in a long time. Although she was never going to see him again it was fun to dream. What would tomorrow bring?

★   ★   ★

In bed that night Megan thought she could hear raised voices. At first she imagined it might be coming from the street below, before realising it was her sister and Tom, but they were too far away to make out what was being said.

Not wishing to intrude on something private, Megan willed herself to switch off and try to sleep.

'Was everything all right last night?' she asked Sarah next morning.

'Of course,' Sarah said brightly. She didn't seem in the least bit distressed so Megan didn't push. It was none of her business. Anyway she was in a hurry to get to the Louvre early to beat the crowds.

She was so early there was barely any queue at all — only a group of American students with backpacks and a couple of Japanese tourists. Sunlight glinted off the tip of the glass pyramid and deep shadows shrouded the edge of the courtyard.

Once inside Megan set out for the portrait gallery where she stood in front of Hyacinthe Rigaud's painting of Louis XIV. She was scrutinising it, trying to access the real man behind the image, when her mobile phone began to hum. Megan retrieved it from her bag. She frowned when she saw the number: it was school.

'Hello?'

'Megan, Gillian here. Sorry to bother you on holiday.'

'That's okay,' Megan told the head. 'I'm actually in the Louvre at the moment.'

'Ah wonderful.' Gillian Tate sighed. 'I knew you were in Paris. That's why I've called you, actually. I've had a concerned phone call about one of the Year

Nines, Lulu Santerre.'

Megan knew who she meant immediately — the fourteen-year-old French girl with the boyish haircut.

'Her guardian rang me yesterday. He's worried she won't be returning in the Autumn, some personal problem he's not aware of. I told him you were on holiday in the city and would call. Would you mind?'

Megan scribbled down the phone number and an address in the upmarket Eiffel Tower quarter of the city.

'I'm so grateful to you, Megan,' the head did sound relieved.

'I'm here anyway,' Megan reassured her. 'It'll be no hardship to call. I'll let you know what happens.'

People were beginning to drift into the room as she found a seat by the window and tapped in the phone number. She glanced down into the courtyard as she waited for an answer, the queue was longer now.

'Bonjour,' a man's voice said. 'Raphael Santerre.'

'Hello. Is that Lulu Santerre's guardian?'

'Oui.'

Megan quickly explained about who she was and why she was calling.

'Ah, thank you for your quick response. I am worried.' Raphael Santerre's English was perfect, she noticed.

'May I call to see Lulu?'

'Of course. I am home today. Will you call this afternoon? At three?'

Appointment made, Megan resumed her tour. She wasn't so much interested in the exhibits as the building itself. Notebook in hand, she recorded its layouts and features.

Out on the street again she found somewhere to lunch at a pavement table and watch the world go by. It was all such a contrast to the quiet, genteel world of Winhampton College surrounded by flat, rolling fields with the small hamlet of Filburgh a mile down the road. She felt like she was part of civilisation again. She'd missed the buzz of city life.

★ ★ ★

Megan was ten minutes early when she turned up at the address Gillian had passed on to her, part of a handsome four-storey terrace on a tree-lined boulevard with intricate ironwork balconies and grey wooden shutters at the windows.

She climbed steps from the street and rang the bell at the side of a set of imposing black doors.

'Bonjour, Madame.' A gruff expression greeted her, as if its owner was suspicious of anyone who called at the door.

'Bonjour, je m'appelle Megan Honeyman,' she said, and explained in her stumbling French why she'd come.

The butler, if he was a butler, looked down his nose at her, but nodded and invited her in. Megan stepped into a cool hallway, looking around in wonder at the gilded mirrors, the marble floor and the Louis XV chairs. Through open doors she could see another hallway with a sweeping staircase.

'Madame?' The butler was waiting for her at a door to the left.

'Sorry, it's such a wonderful house!'

The observation didn't appear to impress him.

'Wait here, please,' he instructed, showing her into an elegant room. Heavy silk brocade curtains hung at the huge windows, in front of white blinds pulled halfway down to keep out the glare of the sun. The mellow floorboards creaked as she moved across the room.

Megan paused at a polished mahogany writing desk covered with family photographs. There was Lulu and . . . She held her breath. Didn't she recognise that face?

'Bonjour Madame. I am grateful you agreed to come.'

Megan turned quickly. Framed in the doorway stood a tall, slim man, casually dressed in well-cut slacks and a cashmere black polo neck jumper, dark hair brushing his shoulders. She swallowed an 'oh'.

'I am Raphael Santerre, Lulu's brother and official guardian,' he came into the room and extended a hand in greeting.

It was the man she'd bumped into at the Hall of Mirrors.

3

Raphael Santerre frowned as he stepped forward to greet Megan.

'Don't I know you?' he said

'The palace yesterday.' She was certain she was grinning like a Cheshire cat and tried to control herself.

'Ah yes,' he smiled. 'We bumped into each other. You were not hurt?'

'No, not at all. It was clumsy of me.'

An older woman appeared in the doorway carrying a tray.

'Afternoon tea?' Raphael Santerre offered. 'I know how you English enjoy your tea.'

The woman placed the tray on a large stool in front of the marble fireplace and silently withdrew.

Megan sat in one of the striped silk chairs and watched the man pour. The faint smell of coconut and vanilla hovered in the air.

'So you are Mademoiselle Honey-man.'

She took the cup and saucer, trying not to stare into her host's dark eyes.

'Lulu speaks of you. You teach History, non?'

She nodded.

'And tennis. Lulu likes tennis.'

'Does she?' Megan hadn't especially noticed that at school.

'Or so she tells me.'

He sat in the chair opposite, gave her a long, considered look.

'I didn't know Lulu had a brother,' Megan said quickly, looking down into her teacup and hoping she wasn't going to blush like a teenager during this professional conversation. 'You're her guardian?'

'I was her age when she was born,' Raphael Santerre explained. 'Our mother died seven years ago — cancer. Our father died a year last May, a boating accident on the Cote d'Azur. As Lulu is a minor I became her legal guardian.'

'I wasn't aware of that. Lulu's not under my pastoral care at school.'

'Miss Tate assured me you would be able to help.'

Gillian Tate displayed premature confidence, Megan mused.

'What's the problem?' she asked.

'Teenage rebellion,' Raphael Santerre replaced his cup and saucer on the tray and sat back in his chair, clasping his hands together.

'She doesn't want to return to school in the autumn.'

'A common complaint.' Megan tried to concentrate. This wasn't like any parents' meeting she'd had at school. 'If you don't mind me asking, why is Lulu at Winhampton? It's a long way from home.'

'It was our mother's old school,' Raphael explained. 'She was English — Charlotte Hamford. She always wanted Lulu to go to Winhampton. After she died, Papa merely carried out her wishes.'

'As far as I'm aware Lulu's not

unhappy. You get to hear of any problems with the pupils in the staff-room. Lulu's name has never come up in that context.' Megan looked into her cup as if she might find an answer there. 'Perhaps the death of her father has stirred up unresolved feelings over her mother's death. It's not easy for a young teenager who finds herself an orphan, especially with all those raging hormones.'

'You may be right,' Raphael agreed. 'I suspect also she has a boyfriend here in Paris and doesn't want to leave him.'

'At fourteen? When would she see him if she's never here?'

He smiled. 'French women have ways.'

She was sure French men had ways too and she blushed at the thought.

'I don't think Lulu has many friends,' Raphael said. 'Not in Paris.'

Come to think of it, Megan didn't believe she had any friends in school either, not close friends. There was an aloofness to Lulu Santerre.

Megan heard the front door opening then slam, the echo reverberating around the grand baroque hallway. Raphael suddenly sat forward in his chair and called out: 'Lulu, c-est tu? Venez ici!'

Lulu, when she appeared a moment later, was not dressed for a hot August afternoon, yet she still looked chic in her long-sleeved jersey top, waistcoat, short pleated skirt, thick tights and clumpy boots.

'Q'est-ce que c'est?' she began, then froze when she saw Megan.

'Hello, Lulu.'

'Madame Honeyman is in Paris on holiday,' Raphael explained.

'Mademoiselle, actually,' Megan felt compelled to set him straight.

'My apologies,' he inclined his head.

'Come and talk to us.' He beckoned to his sister.

Megan could tell the teenager didn't want to but her exquisite manners prevailed. Lulu sat down on the sofa, crossing her legs neatly at the ankles despite the clunky boots, and placing her hands in her lap.

'How are you, Mademoiselle Honeyman?' she asked politely.

'I'm very well, Lulu, how are you?' Megan smiled.

'Bien,' she shrugged. The question 'Why are you here?' was in her eyes although she did not utter it.

'I've spoken with your head teacher,' Raphael informed his sister.

She clicked her tongue impatiently.

'I told you I would,' he continued. 'As Mademoiselle Honeyman is on holiday in Paris Madame Tate asked her to call.' He sighed. 'I know there's something wrong, Lulu. If you won't talk to me then maybe you'll talk to Mademoiselle Honeyman.' And with that he got up, excused himself and left them alone.

Raphael Santerre was assuming a lot, Megan thought, slightly miffed, as she tried to smile encouragingly at the sullen girl.

With her brother gone, Lulu became more vocal and less polite.

'It was not necessary for you to call,' she got up from the sofa and folded her arms aggressively. 'I'm not in school now.'

'No, I quite agree,' Megan sought to sound reasonable. 'If I were you I wouldn't like it either. I'm on holiday, too, and I don't particularly want to be dealing with school business.'

Lulu's confrontational stance relaxed a little. Then she frowned.

'I don't know why Rapha has to interfere,' she said, rubbing her chin. 'It's my life. So what if I don't want to go back to England?'

'Are you having any problems at school? Are you being bullied? Have you spoken to your house mistress?'

'There's nothing to speak about. I'm sorry my brother's brought you here, Mademoiselle. I make my own decisions and he can't stop me,' she spread her hands in regret. 'Excuse me.'

Megan got up as the girl hastened

out of the room. Well, that wasn't very successful, she reflected. What should she do now? It seemed odd to just walk out without telling anyone.

★　★　★

The hallway was deserted as Megan stepped out. She peered into a room opposite, filled with Louis XV furniture, its walls lined with olive silk. Then she made her way into the second hallway where the grand staircase swept up three floors to a cupola that splashed sunlight into a pool on the marble floor. All was silent.

Tentatively, Megan wandered off to the left. The first door she opened revealed a library, again empty. Something made her knock at the second door, and a voice she recognised bade her enter.

She found herself in a remarkably modern study containing a sparse streamlined desk behind which Raphael sat tapping away on a laptop.

'Mademoiselle?' He looked up, surprised.

'I'm sorry,' she said. 'Lulu wouldn't talk. I didn't want to leave without letting anyone know.'

'Of course,' he waved her in. 'I'm sorry that Lulu was rude,' Raphael got up from his chair. 'I shall speak to her.'

'Oh, no, she wasn't rude, just reticent,' Megan said quickly. 'And probably put out that she has to see a teacher during her holidays.'

'It is not good enough,' he shook his head.

'Perhaps you could tell me more,' Megan encouraged him.

He shot a quick glance at his watch.

'Not now,' he said. 'We should arrange to meet again.' He took in Megan's dubious expression. 'This time I will make it seem more like pleasure than business,' he assured her. 'Would you like to join me for dinner one evening?'

'Oh, yes! — I mean . . . That would be acceptable,' she said, flustered.

'Tomorrow night?'

'Yes, I believe I'm free.' She'd jolly well make sure she was!

'May I send a car for you?'

'If you must.'

She told him her sister's address and he tapped it into his BlackBerry.

'I will send for you at 7.30,' he said, walking her to the door.

Out on the street again Megan had to pause. What had just happened? The dreamy Hall of Mirrors man has asked her on a date! Well, not exactly a date, but still . . . She smiled as she set off back to Sarah's. The holiday was looking up and it was only her second day.

★ ★ ★

'I couldn't believe that Lulu's guardian turned out to be that divine man I bumped into at Versailles yesterday — the one I was telling you about.' Megan concluded her tale to her sister as they sipped pre-dinner drinks and waited for Tom to arrive home. 'I'm beginning to think fate is on my side.'

Sarah pulled a face. 'You don't know anything about him. You have to be careful with French men; they can really turn on the charm.'

'We're only having dinner to discuss Lulu,' Megan protested.

She didn't like the way Sarah wrinkled up her nose. Megan recognised the jealousy of old. It had been obvious as Megan had described the house. The Santerres were old money with property, whereas Sarah and Tom were renting their apartment and struggling to find a foothold in French society. Sarah had always been the successful one and to have Megan moving in more exalted circles was an unwelcome development.

'Is everything all right with you and Tom?' Megan asked suddenly.

'Of course, why wouldn't it be?' Sarah looked surprised.

'You were arguing last night.'

'It's what couples do.'

'Okay. But if there's something bothering you, remember, I'm your sister and I'm here for you.'

'Nothing's wrong,' Sarah said tersely and rose from her chair. 'Speaking of Tom, I'd better check with Madame Boursin, see how dinner's coming along.'

But Megan noticed that as she left, Sarah topped up her glass.

4

The next day, Megan agonised for hours over what to wear. Finally she was ready. Tom looked up from his paper as she entered the room.

'I hear you're not eating with us this evening,' he said. 'Sarah says you've got a meeting with a pupil's father.'

'Brother,' Megan corrected him. 'He's her legal guardian. You're a man, what do you think?' She gave him a twirl. 'Not too 'we're on a date' is it? And not too school mistress either?' She looked at him uncertainly. She'd finally teamed her demure black dress with a low heeled court shoe and a grey angora cardigan.

'You look nice, just right,' Tom grinned. 'Gives out all the right signals. I'd be interested.'

'Interested in what?' Sarah joined them from the kitchen.

41

'Just asking Tom what he thought of my outfit,' Megan brushed the fabric over her stomach; she really ought to be careful with the French pastries over the next few weeks.

Sarah looked her up and down.

'It needs some pearls to finish it off,' she said sagely.

'It's not a date,' Megan reminded her.

'No, but pearls are chic. They make a statement. Let me get mine.'

'So how are you doing Tom? How's work?' Megan perched on the arm of the sofa as she waited for Sarah to return.

He folded his newspaper and laid it aside on an occasional table beside his chair. Megan noted the tumbler of whisky, generously filled.

'The usual,' he rubbed the back of his neck then sat back with a sigh. 'Takeover fears are rife at the moment, loans being called in, bit of a dodgy time in the markets.'

'You'll be okay though, right?'

'Honestly?' He glanced toward the door to make sure Sarah had really gone. 'I don't know how it's going to pan out Megs, or if I'll even have a job at the end of the summer. I haven't told Sarah, I don't want to alarm her unnecessarily. She loves the apartment, the parties, her job. I can't see her wanting to leave Paris.'

'I've heard you arguing,' Megan confessed.

'That's over other things. This work thing would just be the last straw.' He reached for the tumbler of whisky. 'I'll find something else, but we might have to go back to the US and I know Sarah's already mentally spent the bonus she's expecting me to get.'

'I'm sorry Tom. I didn't realise.'

'It's not your problem.' He smiled. 'And I shouldn't have told you. Hey, you're on vacation.'

'Listen, I'm going to be listening to somebody else's problems tonight,' Megan grinned. 'I'm getting used to it.'

Sarah reappeared then.

'Here they are,' she offered a string of milky white pearls. 'Tom gave them to me on our first wedding anniversary. You don't mind, darling, do you?' She glanced at her husband.

'Go ahead.' He winked at Megan.

After she'd fastened the pearls about her throat, Megan admired her reflection in the mirrored panels between the windows. Yes, they did set off the dress; not too showy, yet sophisticated.

'Now I can show Monsieur Raphael Santerre that I mean business.' She turned to face them just as the doorbell rang. 'Must be the car.' Megan grabbed her bag. 'I won't be late, but I've got the key just in case.'

'You do remember how to set the alarm?' Sarah said anxiously.

'It'll be fine,' Megan assured her, already at the door.

'Mademoiselle Honeyman?' said the driver, who was waiting on the step. Megan followed him to a BMW parked at the kerb. He opened the door and she climbed into the plush recesses of the back seat.

It beat the Metro, Megan smiled to herself as they negotiated the Parisian evening traffic. Lights were coming on everywhere as dusk fell, the city took on new life, as floodlit monuments and buildings shook off their daytime aspect. They drove along the Rue de Rivoli, through the Place de la Concorde, in a maelstrom of beeping traffic.

Eventually Megan lost any sense of where they were going as the car travelled through a labyrinth of boulevards and backstreets. Half an hour later it drew up in front of a canopied entrance and Megan waited for the chauffeur to open the door for her.

'If you ask the Maitre d' for Monsieur Santerre's table,' he said. 'He asked me to inform you he may be a little delayed.'

Megan wasn't used to walking into restaurants as fine as this, but as soon as she gave her name the Maitre d' beamed warmly and signalled for her to follow him: 'This way Mademoiselle.'

Megan followed him across the chandeliered room past the tables of impossibly elegant diners, to a table in a corner.

'May I bring you an aperitif?' He held out the chair for her.

'Just some water please.'

Left alone Megan glanced around; this was definitely not the sort of place she felt at home in, but it was a new experience and she was determined to enjoy herself.

'Perhaps mademoiselle would like to see the menu while she is waiting?' A waiter appeared at her shoulder.

Megan took the embossed book from him and raised an eyebrow. She couldn't see any prices on any of the pages, and didn't dare ask.

The waiter brought her water. She sipped it quickly to lubricate her throat which had suddenly become dry, then looked around again. How long was Raphael Santerre going to keep her waiting? Not long as it turned out, for he suddenly appeared, weaving his way through the tables, looking as enticing as the last time she'd seen him.

He apologised for keeping her waiting, then leaned over to kiss her on both cheeks — not the sort of greeting she normally received at a parent/teacher consultation, Megan reflected in amusement.

He acccpted a menu from the attentive waiter. Megan watched him as he read. He pursed his lips, the dark eyes serious, then he looked up and smiled when he'd made his selection. Almost immediately the waiter was at the table taking their orders. Raphael ordered wine.

'Have you had a good day?' he asked, sitting back in his chair.

'Yes. I spent it at the Musée Carnavalet. It was quiet. I suppose most of the tourists head for the Louvre or the d'Orsay.'

'It's one of our hidden gems.' He nodded. 'So, you are not a tourist?'

'Actually, I'm doing research,' said Megan. 'I have a passion for Louis XIV,

I've wanted to write a novel forever. Now that I'm in Paris I thought I'd hunt out the baroque, get a flavour of the times.'

He raised an eyebrow. 'What do you like about Louis Quatorze?'

'There are very few people who are born to a role which fits them perfectly,' Megan reflected. 'Especially when it comes to power. He made the office his own.'

'The Sun King,' Raphael paused. 'We French are divided of course.'

'Well, you did have a revolution.'

'And even when we returned to monarchy it never really worked for us, unlike you English.'

'We seem to like the pomp and fripperies.' She grinned.

The wine arrived. Raphael tasted it, nodded and the waiter poured.

As they waited for their meal conversation turned to Winhampton College, and how Megan had come to teach there. She chose not to mention Dev.

'I thought Lulu was happy there.' Raphael sighed. 'She never objected to going to England in the first place.'

'You said she might have a boyfriend she doesn't want to leave,' Their food arrived and Megan picked up her fork.

'I believe so, although she hasn't spoken of anyone.'

'Perhaps something else is making her want to stay in Paris,' Megan suggested. 'Something, or someone she's worried about?'

'I don't think so, Mademoiselle . . . '

'You can call me Megan, if it's okay with you. I know we're having a guardian/teacher discussion, but Mademoiselle sounds so formal.'

He nodded, but didn't invite her to call him by his first name.

'She wouldn't talk to me at all,' Megan continued. 'She appeared to resent the intrusion into her holiday time.'

'But you could try again,' he said hopefully.

Megan hesitated. The idea was

appealing, not so much because of Lulu, but rather the man she faced across the table. She noted the contrast of the collar of his shirt against tanned skin, the masculine watch, the exquisitely tailored suit, the way a stray strand of hair fell into his eyes, the confidence and ease with which he related to the waiter.

She glanced around the room and through the window to the well-lit street beyond. She was in Paris, in an exclusive restaurant having dinner with a handsome man, when only the other day she'd been dining in the school refectory with its unique aroma of cabbage and sponge. If this was the life Lulu was used to, she could begin to understand her reluctance to return. She almost didn't want to go back herself.

'It's been difficult for Lulu. It's especially hard for a girl to be without a mother when she becomes a teenager,' Raphael continued.

'What about you; how are you

managing without your parents?' The intrusive question was out before Megan could stop herself.

'I was older.' He smiled sadly. 'It didn't affect me so much.'

'But you only lost your father last year.'

'I've been busy taking over his affairs. Life goes on.' He shrugged and offered her some more wine.

'Just a little,' Megan said, this was a professional meeting, after all.

'So you went to Versailles the other day because of Louis Quatorze,' Raphael replenished his wine glass.

'I thought I could sneak in when everyone had left. I wanted to get the true ambience of the place and it's a little hard to do that when it's packed with twenty-first century tourists.'

'If you like, I could arrange a private viewing for you.'

Megan stopped with her wine glass halfway to her lips. She knew she was gaping like a fish but couldn't help herself.

'I have connections,' Raphael explained. 'I'll make a call.'

'Oh!' Megan put a hand to her mouth to stifle a delighted laugh. 'That would be amazing!'

'Remember, I'm a businessman, I drive a hard bargain,' he cautioned her. 'In return you will speak with Lulu again.'

'Done!' Megan didn't even have to think about it. She extended a hand across the table and they shook on the deal.

They moved on to dessert and Raphael told her about his family, originally from the Loire Valley where they still had a chateau near Amboise.

'Grandfather was a wine merchant, but my father expanded into other areas and now the family has varied business interests around the world.'

'By family, you mean you?' Megan tackled her profiteroles, trying to do them justice without getting cream or chocolate over her face.

'Sometimes I think it would be nice

to go back to wine,' he said wistfully. 'Back to Amboise.'

'Perhaps Lulu would like that?'

'I think Lulu likes Paris. All young girls like Paris.'

'I can't argue with that,' Megan agreed. She was beginning to feel comfortably relaxed. She reflected how much easier it was to get to know someone when you had a mutual interest. Of course, most pupils didn't have single brothers who looked as if they could have stepped off the pages of a magazine. She chuckled to herself.

'What amuses you?'

'Sorry. I was just thinking of something to do with school,' she apologised, pushing her wine glass out of reach; she was not going to let it go to her head.

'Coffee?' Raphael suggested.

He called for the waiter, and presently coffee arrived. Megan was pondering why Raphael had asked for three cups when a woman approached their table. Raphael rose from his chair to greet her with a kiss on each cheek.

'Darling,' she said.

'Just in time for coffee, as you said,' he pulled away. 'This is Mademoiselle Honeyman, the teacher from Lulu's school I was telling you about.'

'Enchanté.'

'Hi, I'm Megan,' Megan said, offering her hand.

'This is Maryam d'Aneste,' Raphael smiled. 'My girlfriend.'

The woman had startling blue eyes, which were turned on Megan with an unmistakable 'No trespassing' expression. Effortlessly stylish, in a crisply tailored black suit, a row of pearls visible at the open neck of her white blouse, her perfectly-coiffed blonde chignon, red lips and manicured nails left Megan feeling almost scruffy by comparison.

'The traffic over Pont Alexandre III was terrible.' Maryam d'Aneste sighed as Raphael held out a chair and she slipped gracefully into it.

'But you closed the deal?' he asked.

'Mais, oui.' Her generous lips parted in a smile. 'And I told you I would get here in time for coffee.' She laid a hand on Raphael's arm. No engagement ring, Megan noticed.

'Did you resolve the problem with Lulu?'

'Not yet,' said Raphael.

'Teenage girls.' Maryam d'Aneste threw a cold and haughty smile in Megan's direction.

'I'm sure we'll get to the bottom of it,' Megan said. There was something in the tone of the woman's voice which made her feel uneasy.

The woman raised a surprised eyebrow.

'I've asked Megan to speak with Lulu again,' Raphael explained.

'I can't see the point, cheri. She's a teenage girl. It's her hormones'

Megan drank her coffee feeling awkward now. Of course she should have known that a man like Raphael Santerre would have someone. What was she thinking? She'd let her imagination run away with her. She finished her coffee quickly and glanced at her watch.

'I should be getting back,' she said. 'Thank you for a wonderful meal.'

'Let me walk you to the car,' Raphael said, getting up. 'Henri's waiting outside. He'll drive you home.'

'I can take the Metro.'

'I can't let you do that.' He flipped open his phone and called the chauffeur then walked her to the entrance where the car was pulling up.

'I will make the arrangements for the chateau,' he said, holding the door open for her.

For a split second she thought he meant the chateau at Amboise.

'Enjoy your visit to Versailles. May I call you in a couple of days and we will talk of Lulu again?'

'I'll be waiting.'

★ ★ ★

'How did it go?' Sarah asked as Megan sauntered into the drawing room. Her

56

sister was reading a book and nursing a glass of wine.

'Posh place, nice food.'

'Where was it?'

'Gils Dupuis.'

'You lucky thing!' Sarah looked envious. 'I've been nagging Tom for ages to get us a reservation there.'

'Are you going to see him again?'

Megan collapsed into an armchair and sighed. 'He wants me to talk to Lulu again. And he's promised me a private view of the Hall of Mirrors.'

Sarah raised an impressed eyebrow.

'Things seem to be looking up for you,' she said. 'All your past boyfriends have been dead losses; now here's a man who is someone.'

'Thanks, Sarah.'

'No, I mean none of them had any prospects. Even Dev.'

'I don't care about all that stuff.'

'That's the difference between us.' Sarah took a sip of her wine.

'Anyway, it's not going to happen,' Megan picked at the velvet fabric on the arm of her chair. 'He's got a girlfriend. She joined us for coffee. She's a high-flier, too, blonde, beautiful, impossibly elegant. I'm just his sister's school teacher.'

'Oh, what a pity,' Sarah sighed. 'I told you you had to be careful of a Frenchman's charm. They do know how to turn it on.'

'I was never caught up in him anyway,' Megan patted the arm of the chair, then got up. 'It was just a physical attraction, a nice thing to dream about.' She stretched. 'I think I'll go to bed.'

'What about tomorrow?' Sarah said. 'It's Saturday. I thought we might go shopping.'

'Okay.' It seemed a good idea to spend some time together. 'Thanks for these by the way.' Megan unclasped the string of pearls and placed them into Sarah's outstretched hand.

'Don't get up too early,' Sarah advised as Megan left the room.

Well, that was going to be impossible; she was still on school time.

5

Sarah insisted they window-shop along the Rue du Faubourg Saint-Honoré and all the designer shops in the surrounding area.

'Even I don't get to go in these,' she said sadly. 'Well, maybe once a year, but Tom can be pretty stingy.'

'That's not a bad thing,' said Megan, thinking of what he'd told her.

Sarah rolled her eyes. 'Trust you. You've just never had aspirations.'

Not to the sort of lifestyle Sarah coveted. It wasn't that she didn't like nice things, but Megan had always preferred to save her money for travel or experiences than spend it on stuff that she would soon get bored of or on clothes she might only wear once or twice. Even as a child she'd lived in jeans while Sarah had spent every penny she earned on the latest looks.

'It's like a permanent catwalk,' she commented to her sister as yet another raven-haired beauty in belted jacket and slim trousers glided by.

'Parisian women just seem to have the knack,' Sarah agreed. 'I've been taking tips from Chloe at the gallery. She's recommended a lot of the stuff I buy.'

Megan gave her sister an appraising look. She didn't look out of place among these elegant Parisiennes. Maybe she would pick up some ideas herself, although she couldn't imagine achieving the effortless style of someone like Maryam d'Aneste. After an hour of traipsing exclusive streets she'd had enough and suggested they go to Galeries Lafayette.'

'You're so bourgeois.' Sarah sighed. 'Actually,' she admitted with a grin, 'I quite like it myself.'

The sisters spent another hour wandering around the busy department store. Megan bought a silk scarf of intermingled blue tones.

'It suits your colouring,' Sarah approved.

'This is nice,' Megan said as they strolled through the lingerie department. 'We've hardly seen each other the past year and we've never done things together really. It's nice to be like sisters.'

Sarah grunted a reply, turning her attention to a red silk and lace bra.

'I think Tom would like this,' she said.

'Too much information,' Megan grimaced and turned away.

All these flimsy bits of lace and silk on hangers. It was all right if you had someone to wear them for, otherwise why would you bother? She wondered if she'd want to buy this sort of stuff if things developed between her and Mike Havers, but couldn't imagine it, some-how.

'I think I'll buy this,' said Sarah.

★ ★ ★

'How long do you think you and Tom will stay in Paris?' Megan broached the subject as they sat outside at a pavement café. They'd found a quiet side street and ordered coffee and pastries. A faint breeze ruffled the overhead canopy, a respite from the heat of the day.

'As long as we can, I hope. I love my job.'

'And how does Tom feel about it?' Megan probed.

'Oh you know what it's like in this climate — there are always rumours of cutbacks. He's pretty secure though.'

Unwilling to betray a confidence, Megan decided to drop the subject. Anyway it was up to Tom to let his wife know what was really going on.

'Sometimes he gets homesick,' Sarah said suddenly. 'He's been talking more about home lately.' She toyed with her spoon. 'But really, how can Boston compare with Paris?'

'I like Boston,' said Megan. She'd stayed there for a week when Tom and Sarah got married four years before, and then travelled down to New York for a few days.

'You go and deal with his family then.' Sarah muttered darkly.

'What's wrong with them?'

Sarah shrugged. 'Oh, nothing, really. It's just that Tom's sisters have produced children and James and Mindy want to know when Tom and I are going to add to the tally of grandchildren. There's always pressure.'

'Tom sounds keen,' Megan bit into a confection of pastry and cream. Pastry flaked everywhere and cream coated her upper lip. She dabbed at it with a napkin. 'But it sounds like you don't want to try again.'

'I think it was a sign, don't you?' Sarah remarked.

Megan regarded her sister with compassion.

'Do you have any idea how many women miscarry their first baby?' she began.

'And then Mum and Dad died.'

'There was no connection,' Megan said, shocked.

'I know that.'

63

'But you've linked the two in your mind.' Suddenly she understood.

'I've just come to see that bad things happen. I'm not ready. I'm not sure if I'll ever be ready. Maybe it's a good thing I lost the baby; it made me re-evaluate. I don't want to be a mother.' Sarah looked away deliberately into the passing traffic.

Megan studied her sister for a moment — the sharp chin and chiselled cheeks, just a little too hollow, the eyes that never seemed to tell the truth. She looked brittle, Megan thought, projecting an image of a perfect life whilst trying to prevent it shattering.

'We've never really talked about Mum and Dad since the accident.'

'What is there to talk about?' Sarah turned her attention to the cream slice on her plate, cutting it carefully before delicately popping a small piece into her mouth — no cream and pastry over her face and clothes. 'They died on holiday in a car crash.'

'You had Tom to talk to when it

happened, but I had no-one,' Megan reflected. 'I would have valued some-one . . . I would have valued you.'

She remembered how Sarah had come home for the funeral with Tom, how little time the two of them had had to talk. It was a case of making arrangements and sorting out the house quickly after the funeral.

'You had Dev,' her sister said now.

'He was away, if you remember. Come to think of it, when he was in New York he'd probably already started the affair with Cara.'

'You know me, Megan, I've never been good at talking about things.'

'Maybe we should talk now. I'm here and we have all this time together.'

Sarah shrugged and concentrated on her pastry.

'It's obviously affected you, Sarah,' Megan encouraged her.

'Life has to go on, no matter how much you're affected by something,' her sister dismissed it.

'Yes, but you've linked it with the

65

miscarriage and it's stopping you from trying for another baby.'

'You don't know anything about what's been going on and how I feel.'

'So tell me.'

'No, not now, not yet.'

'What about me? I'm your sister. What if I want to talk?'

'Really? Here? On a beautiful sunny day in Paris with life all around you?' Sarah impatiently put down her fork. 'It was three years ago. You should be looking to the future.'

'I'm not going to let it go.'

'Fine.' Sarah threw down her napkin and sat back in her chair. 'But not here. Now, where are we going shopping next?'

Megan conceded that for the moment the subject was closed. They finished their coffee. She was tired of shopping; it all seemed so superficial. She wanted more than anything to reconnect with her sister and somehow come to terms with the deaths of their parents.

A couple of days later Megan had a call from Raphael Santerre.

'I've arranged for you to have a private viewing at the Galerie des Glaces on Wednesday,' he said. 'When you arrive at the chapel entrance around closing time ask for Monsieur Valbonne.'

'Thank you,'

'I have to fly to New York for a few days. Perhaps when I return we can arrange for you to meet Lulu again.'

On Wednesday Megan once more took the train to Versailles, excitement bubbling up as she passed tourists boarding their coaches and taking final photographs.

'Non, Madame,' an official tried to dissuade her from entering. 'Le chateau est fermé.'

'Monsieur Valbonne?' Megan enquired, slipping in through the gate. She explained about the arrangement, pleased that her French was holding up. At her mention of Raphael the woman nodded and invited Megan to follow her.

They traversed the now empty courtyard and entered the palace, their footsteps echoing in the space in a way they never could when the palace was full of people.

'Monsieur Valbonne?' The woman hailed a small, neat man with a moustache. His face broke into a bright smile.

'Mademoiselle Honeyman? Welcome.'

Megan shook his hand.

'I'm very grateful,' she said sincerely.

'Non, c'est mon plaisir. Pour Monsieur Santerre. Now you must understand we cannot allow you to wander the chateau freely, but come, I will take you through the state apartments to the Grande Galerie.'

Megan followed him up a flight of stairs to arrive in the north wing and the first of the state rooms, seeing them properly for the first time now they were emptied of people. Only the occasional guide tidying up at the end of the day remained.

When they came to the Hall of Mirrors Monsieur Valbonne held back so that she might walk alone into the room. Megan paused at a window and looked out over the gardens. The sun was setting over the trees beyond the grand canal, bathing the room in a golden glow. She could smell the heat of the day, hear the chattering of birds.

Then she drew back and observed herself in a panelled mirror, imagining what it might have been like all those centuries ago when the room was buzzing with courtiers and princes and ambassadors. Megan could almost believe she'd gone back in time until she became aware of Monsieur Valbonne discreetly moving further into the room, following her as she walked in the direction of the south wing. Even people who'd been vouched for had to be watched she supposed.

After a while she turned towards him.

'It's an extraordinary place,' she said.

'We think so,' he smiled. 'Now it is for all the French people to enjoy.' He extended a hand. 'This way please, Mademoiselle to the Queen's apartments.'

It was hotter in the south wing. At the windows opaque white blinds were pulled down three quarters of the way to ward off the bleaching effects of the sun.

'How was Monsieur Santerre able to gain me this access?' Megan asked intrigued as she sauntered through the row of rooms with Monsieur Valbonne at her side.

'Monsieur Santerre is a great friend and patron,' the little man explained. 'We were happy to accede to his request.'

'His sister attends the school where I teach,' Megan suddenly felt the need to explain her connection with Raphael Santerre. 'I'm spending the holiday in Paris with my sister.'

The little man nodded as if to say it was none of his business.

70

'I suppose buildings like these need wealthy patrons,' Megan said.

'The late Monsieur Santerre gave a great deal of money.'

They came to the final room and Megan asked if they could go back so that she might take a last look at the Hall of Mirrors.

'Mais, oui,' Monsieur Valbonne agreed.

Megan was aware that he'd probably finished work for the day and had a home to go to, but she was loathe to leave knowing that she would never have such an opportunity again. In the Hall of Mirrors once again she found herself thinking of Raphael, recalling their first meeting in this very place. A pity he was spoken for; it would have been the stuff of a romantic novel — the single boarding school teacher meeting a charming Frenchman with connections. Ah well, it was not to be.

'I could never grow tired of this place,' Megan sighed. 'I suppose working here every day you must get used to it.'

'Never,' Monsieur Valbonne smiled. 'It is a privilege. Louis Quatorze built a chateau and gardens for the soul as well as for the eyes.'

'He certainly did,' Megan muttered to herself, glancing round again.

'I believe Monsieur Santerre is planning to hold his reception here.'

'Reception?' Megan shot him a sharp look.

'When he and Mademoiselle d'Aneste marry next Easter.'

So Maryam d'Aneste was rather more than a girlfriend.

'I'm sure it will be quite perfect,' she forced herself to say. 'Well, Monsieur, I believe I should be leaving. I am very grateful for your time.'

He shook her hand. 'It was my pleasure.'

Megan took a final long look around the room. She would never see it like this again.

*　*　*

By the time Megan got back to the apartment it was dark and she was ravenous.

'We've eaten,' Sarah said as Megan strolled into the drawing room. Tom was sprawled on the sofa watching television. Sarah sat across from him inspecting a book of photographs by the light of a lamp. 'We've left you some in the kitchen.'

'Thanks.'

'Was it worth it?'

'It was wonderful!' Megan enthused. 'Did you know they do wedding receptions there?'

'I've never heard of that,' Sarah shook her head.

'Or maybe it's just for people with connections,' Megan mused. 'Raphael Santerre is marrying that woman who turned up at the restaurant the other night. They're having their reception there.'

'Well at least you can put him out of your mind now,' Sarah said.

'Yes.' Megan shrugged. 'Listen, do

you mind if I take some time to myself? I need to write up notes before the impressions fade.'

Sarah waved a dismissive hand. Tom grunted, too caught up in some discussion on the TV to really notice.

Megan retrieved her supper from the oven. There was wine in the fridge. She poured out a glass and settled at the island unit, opened her notebook and began to write.

6

Trying to put Raphael Santerre out of her mind, Megan continued her exploration of baroque Paris. She returned to the Louvre, hunted out seventeenth century town houses and paid a visit to Les Invalides. The days were hot. She sat on benches or stone walls and scribbled in her notebook, her hand barely able to keep up with her brain as she wrote.

Then, a week after her visit to Versailles, she received a phone call.

'Megan, how are you?'

'I'm well. Thanks for the private viewing at Versailles. It was one of the best moments of my life. How was your trip to New York?'

'It was business,' he replied. 'I'm glad to be home. Would you like to meet Lulu and me for coffee?'

'Certainly.' She knew now it was

going to be all about Lulu this time.

'If you're free how about three o'clock at the Musée d'Orsay?'

Megan agreed and turned up just before the appointed time to find Raphael and Lulu already waiting in the coffee shop. As Megan observed them from a distance she thought Lulu looked happy enough, speaking animatedly with her brother and smiling frequently.

Raphael saw her first. He rose from his chair.

'Thank you for coming,' he greeted her with a chaste kiss on both cheeks. Megan still found it disconcerting. There was a reason why the English shook hands, she thought, as she tried not to blush.

'My pleasure,' she said, clearing her throat.

Lulu suddenly looked guarded as Megan sat down.

'Hello, Lulu, how are you?'

'I am well,' the teenager answered politely.

Megan thought she looked chic today in a blue shift dress, a fabric flower in her short hair. Then she noticed the clumpy boots on Lulu's feet. There was no doubting she was an individual.

'Lulu's been telling me everything she's been up to while I've been away,' Raphael smiled encouragingly at his sister.

'It's not much at all,' she sat back in her chair and played with the spoon in her saucer.

'Enjoying your holiday I hope,' Megan tried to sound non-threatening. 'Have you been seeing friends?'

'My friends are in school.'

'No boyfriend in Paris?'

Lulu shook her head and Raphael looked surprised.

'And I wouldn't tell you even if there was one,' she said. She sat forward in her chair. 'What did you think of Versailles Mademoiselle?' She deftly turned the conversation away from her.

'It was superb,' Megan smiled. 'I never dreamed I would have the opportunity to be alone in such a place. Isn't it magnificent? And Monsieur Valbonne told me that you're planning to hold your wedding reception there,' Megan looked at Raphael. 'Congratulations. When I met your girlfriend the other night I didn't realise you were engaged.'

'I've known Maryam for years,' he explained. 'And it's not official yet, but Versailles has been pencilled in. Maryam wanted to do it.'

At his side Lulu made a kind of snorting noise.

Raphael looked at his watch.

'I have to go. I have a meeting in La Défense soon. Can I leave you with Lulu?' Before Megan could reply he turned to his sister. 'Perhaps, Lulu, you could accompany Mademoiselle Honeyman around the museum.' He rose from his chair, leaned across the table and planted a kiss on Lulu's head. 'Merci, cherie,' he said. He extended a hand to Megan. 'It was nice to see you again, Mademoiselle.'

She watched his retreating back with regret, wondering if she would ever meet him again.

'So where do you want to start?' Lulu drew her attention back.

'I'm sorry, Lulu, this won't be much fun for you, going around a museum with one of your teachers.' She was on the point of telling the girl not to bother when she realised that Raphael had probably engineered this situation to get his little sister to talk.

Lulu shrugged. 'I don't mind doing it for Rapha,' she said, getting up from the table. 'Besides, I know the d'Orsay well. I love it. Where do you want to start? Most people head for the Impressionists.'

'Sounds good to me,' Megan invited Lulu to lead the way.

She followed her through the levels of the building. As in any museum there was too much to look at and too many people.

'I think your brother is worried about you,' Megan began as they stood in front of Monet's *Blue Water Lilies*. She'd been impressed by how Lulu talked so knowledgeably about the painting, with real passion.

'Phf!' Lulu clicked her fingers.

'There has to be something or why would he go to the trouble of ringing the school? He thinks it might be something to do with a boy?'

Lulu actually laughed.

'Well, is it?'

For a moment there was silence as Lulu appeared to consider the painting. Megan didn't think she was particularly good at teasing confidences out of students. She sighed.

'I'm sorry, Lulu, I'd like to help if I can, but I can't force you to open up to me.'

Megan began to walk away. She'd done her best. She was on holiday after all. Why should she be at the beck and call of the Santerres? So what if Lulu didn't return next term? Students dropped out of school all the time. She'd find another school in Paris and

Winhampton College would soon forget about her. Lulu would grow up and Raphael Santerre would marry Maryam d'Aneste and she wouldn't even be a footnote in his memory.

'Mademoiselle, you like my brother, don't you?'

Megan stopped abruptly.

'That's a strange and rather unwelcome remark,' she blustered.

'No it's not. I can tell you do.'

'Lulu, this isn't an appropriate conversation.'

'You were the one who wanted me to open up. Well, now you know how it feels to be exposed'

The teenager's frank eyes showed that she wasn't playing games. Megan guided her to a vacant bench where they both sat down.

'Your brother is not unattractive,' she admitted. 'Lots of people are attractive. Please don't read anything into that.'

'I'm worried about him.'

Megan raised an eyebrow.

'That's why I don't want to return to

81

England. It's nothing to do with me. I don't want to leave him.'

'Why? What's wrong?'

'I hate her!'

'Who?'

'Maryam d'Aneste. She's not right for my brother.'

There was such an intensity of loathing in Lulu's eyes it took Megan's breath away. She frowned.

'She wants him to be something he's not, to throw around money, to be seen in society.' Lulu wrinkled her nose in distaste.

Megan thought she understood; here was a baby sister suddenly losing the attention of an adored older brother to his girlfriend. It must have been so much harder for Lulu who had so recently lost a father.

'Lulu, I know it must be difficult for you,' she began. 'Your parents have died and Raphael is all you have left . . . '

'I'm not jealous of her if that's what you mean!' Lulu cut in, offended. 'I'm not a child! I know Rapha is going to

82

meet someone and settle down. I want him to.'

'I'm sorry.'

'Just because I'm fourteen!'

'Your brother says he's known Maryam d'Aneste for a long time,' Megan said, trying again. 'So she's not a stranger to you.'

'She's always been hanging around, but she's really got her claws into Rapha since Papa died. It's only because he's wealthy and connected.'

Megan suppressed a smile. Wealth and connections were not Raphael Santerre's only attractive features.

'Rapha doesn't want to be the big businessman,' Lulu toyed with the leather bracelet around her thin wrist. 'He never wanted to take over Papa's companies. I think he wants to go back to Amboise — we have a house there. But Maryam won't let him. She wants to play the hostess in Paris. She wants to be on all the big committees, to be seen as a benefactor. She wants to be invited to the

Presidential Palace!' Lulu snorted. 'Once they're married he'll be so unhappy.'

'Oh, Lulu.' Megan sighed and shook her head.

'You think I'm being silly.' Lulu looked at her accusingly.

'If this is what your brother wants, couldn't you support him? Don't you want him to be happy?'

'But it's not what he wants; he just doesn't know it yet. He needs something to wake him up. That's why I'm not going back to school; I've got to stay around to stop this happening.'

'Lulu, you can't.'

'We'll see about that.' The teenager got up.

'Do you honestly think your brother will give up the woman he's going to marry just to make sure you go back to school?' Megan rose too.

'There are other ways,' Lulu said defiantly. 'I just need to show him the alternatives. Will you help me?'

'What? Lulu, you're being unrealistic.'

'You want me to go back to Winhampton, don't you?'

'Truthfully? I don't mind whether you go to school in England or Paris. It's none of my business.' Megan sighed again. 'I don't know your brother, I don't know his fiancée and I'm certainly not going to meddle in their lives. Now, I think we've finished our tour.'

'Okay,' Lulu agreed casually. She really didn't look at all upset. 'Au revoir, Mademoiselle.'

There was a gleam in Lulu's eye as she turned and walked away and Megan had the strangest feeling that this wasn't the last she would hear of this. She decided to walk back to the apartment. It was still warm and sunny as she strolled along the left bank, shaded by the trees, watching the tourist boats on the river, observing customers at pavement cafes. She crossed the Pont Neuf to the northern side of the city, revelling in its beautiful historical buildings — gothic churches, baroque palaces, classical houses and apartment blocks. Megan couldn't recall another city where the past had seemed so acutely alive, or where she'd felt so much at home.

Now she understood her sister's desire to stay in Paris. Even the language wasn't so daunting; Megan had the feeling that if she stayed long enough she would soon be conversing like a native. But school beckoned in the autumn and it would be back to preparing lessons, marking books and supervising extra-curricular activities. Then when would she find the time to spend with Louis XIV?

By the time she got back to the apartment her feet ached — it had been further than she'd anticipated. Sarah had said she would be working late at the gallery and Tom wasn't home yet.

Megan found the cold supper Madame Boursin had left for her in the fridge and then sat down at the island to write. But she couldn't stop her mind wandering to what Lulu had told her. Megan instinctively disliked Maryam d'Aneste herself. Perhaps it was only jealousy, with her looking so perfect and destroying the illusion of a cosy twosome that night at the restaurant. She knew how silly it had been to construct a fantasy with Raphael Santerre, but hadn't been able to stop herself. Well, it was at an end now. She was here to enjoy Paris, not become embroiled in a family's domestic complications.

★   ★   ★

It seemed that Lulu Santerre wasn't finished with her yet, though. The very next day Raphael called again.

'Am I disturbing you?' he began.

'Not at all,' Megan lied equably. Of course he was disturbing her! He'd disturbed her entire holiday. But how could she be uncivil towards the man who'd arranged a private viewing for her at Versailles?

'Lulu wants to invite you to tea at the

house,' he continued. 'She says you're really helping her. In fact she can't stop saying nice things about you. She's never enthused about any of her teachers before.'

Initially flattered, Megan's suspicions were aroused. What game was Lulu playing now?

'So will you be free today?'

'Er . . . ' she hesitated, knowing what her answer should be.

'I realise this must seem like work for you, Mademoiselle,' Raphael Santerre reverted to formality. 'I'm sorry. Lulu seemed very keen.'

'Yes, I'll be there,' Megan promised, almost regretting it as soon as the words had left her lips. Absently she clicked the phone shut, wondering what on earth she had done.

7

At the appointed time, Megan presented herself at the town house. The same butler answered the door but escorted her into a different drawing room, brighter and smaller than the one she'd been in before.

Lulu and her brother both looked up as she entered.

'Megan, thank you for coming,' Raphael rose to greet her and once again, despite her best intentions, Megan felt her stomach perform a little skip. Lulu gave her a sweet smile.

'I've been baking, Mademoiselle,' she said. 'Please try a cupcake.'

Megan sat down, watched as Lulu played host pouring the tea, setting a cake on a plate for her along with a knife and a napkin, her movements elegant and precise.

'I thought afternoon tea might make

you feel at home,' Lulu smiled.

'Thank you Lulu,' Megan said. 'That's very considerate of you.'

She bit into the cupcake; it was delicious.

'You have hidden talents,' she enthused.

'I suppose we all do, Mademoiselle,' Lulu said demurely. 'My brother likes to paint but he doesn't often get the chance these days.'

Megan looked at Raphael. He hadn't reacted to his sister's comment.

'Maryam thinks it's a waste of time though, doesn't she? You used to paint all the time, Rapha, when you were younger.'

'I don't think Mademoiselle Honeyman wants to hear about that,' he looked at his sister, puzzled now.

'No, it sounds interesting,' Megan encouraged him.

'You see, you have something in common — a writer and a painter,' Lulu pronounced, satisfied. 'And Rapha thought about teaching overseas once. Weren't you going to go to Haiti?' Lulu prompted. 'But Papa said he needed you to help with the business.'

Megan looked at him, surprised.

'I'm sure Mademoiselle Honeyman didn't come here to talk about me,' Raphael shook his head at his sister.

'Well I can hardly talk about Mademoiselle Honeyman. She's my teacher,' Lulu returned. 'How are you enjoying your holiday Mademoiselle?' she asked politely, as if changing the subject.

'Paris is a beautiful city.' Megan sipped her tea. 'I could live here quite happily.'

'It would be good for you to leave that stuffy school.'

'Lulu!' Raphael chided. 'How rude!'

'Come and live in Paris,' Lulu persisted. 'Perhaps when you've written your book and it's published you'll be rich. You can come and live near us.'

She turned to her brother and smiled sweetly. 'It's only because I like Mademoiselle Honeyman. You like her, too, don't you Rapha?'

Raphael cleared his throat.

'Lulu, you and I barely know each other,' Megan said quickly to cover her embarrassment. 'I don't think you can like me or not.'

'You like me though, don't you?' Lulu's smile was sly.

'You're a fine young woman.'

'And my brother — you like him.'

'Lulu!' Raphael sounded angry now. 'I apologise for my sister,' he said, turning to Megan.

'Don't worry,' she replied. 'I'm used to teenage girls.'

She was beginning to think she ought to leave when Lulu got up.

'I have something I want to show you, Mademoiselle. Excuse me.'

And then she was gone and Megan was left alone with Raphael.

'Once again, I apologise,' he shook his head. 'Since our father's death Lulu has become quite — shall we say — unpredictable.'

'It's hard for her,' Megan picked up her cup and saucer and took a sip of the rapidly cooling tea. 'Especially now, with no mother to talk to.'

'I was hoping Maryam would help her through this period but,' he shrugged, 'Lulu doesn't seem to want to get close.'

Megan said nothing of what Lulu had told her about Maryam d'Aneste.

'I know what it's like to lose both parents,' she said.

'You do?' He looked surprised.

'Mine died three years ago in a car accident when they were on holiday in Italy. It's hard enough being orphaned when you're an adult, but for a child . . . ' she left the rest unsaid.

'How have you coped?' He leaned forward in his chair, concerned.

'I just got on with life.' Megan shrugged. 'My sister and I haven't really talked about it. Once the funeral was over Sarah just wanted to put it behind her. She'd recently had a miscarriage and it was all too much.'

'I'm sorry.'

'We've had a rough few years.'

'You had no-one to be with, to offer comfort?'

Megan gave a cynical smile. 'I was with someone at the time. His name was Dev. We were about to take a year off to go travelling and then he told me he'd met someone else. I'd given up my job, my home, ready to go. That's when I got the job at the school. It was a roof over my head, somewhere to be and not think too much.'

Even as she spoke about it all those old feelings of displacement and abandonment came rushing back. Quickly she reached out for what was left of the cupcake, and popped it into her mouth so she wouldn't have to say any more. She'd already said too much. Raphael Santerre wasn't really interested in the problems of his sister's school teacher.

But he nodded as if he understood. 'Our father's death was sudden. I've been left to sort out the business.'

'When you might prefer painting and trading in wine at your chateau at

94

Amboise,' Megan swallowed the last few crumbs.

'Maybe you understand me,' he smiled.

'I just think there's a fellowship of the bereaved,' said Megan. 'It's particularly true when you've lost parents at a young age, been forced to grow up. You realise you're next in line.'

'C'est vrai,' he agreed.

'At least you have your fiancée,' Megan dabbed at her mouth with the napkin. 'Lulu tells me you've known each other a long time.'

'We moved in the same circles when we were growing up,' Raphael nodded. 'Then she moved to the south. We met up again at a dinner reception when she returned to Paris just over a year ago.'

'She's very beautiful.'

'And very clever,' he smiled.

When he smiled the edges of his eyes creased; it made him look even more attractive Megan thought.

'Perhaps when you're married you'll move to Amboise,' she suggested.

'I seriously doubt that. Maryam's a city girl. She loves Paris, all the committees and events. She'll expect us to continue our patronage. There'll be no escaping the social round I'm afraid.'

Did he sound regretful? Megan wondered. Is that why Lulu was so worried — that her brother was denying his heart?

'And what will you do, Megan?' He interrupted her train of thought. 'Is teaching a lifetime's vocation?'

'No,' she was quite definite about that. 'It's a stop-gap for now.'

'Maybe Louis Quatorze will be your inspiration,' he said.

'I'll probably never find a publisher, even if I do finish my book,' she said.

'I would like to read it.'

She could feel herself blushing again. Before she could respond, Lulu reappeared, a look of expectation on her face.

'Well?' Raphael enquired.

'Well?' she reiterated, then shrugged.

'Oh, I forgot. Well, I couldn't find it,' she waved a dismissive hand. 'But you talked, yes?'

Megan had suspected all along that it had been a ruse. It wasn't going to work on her, nor on Raphael. She felt sorry for the girl.

'I really must be going.' She got up briskly, replacing her cup and saucer on the tray.

Lulu darted forward, disappointed.

'Stay, Mademoiselle!'

'No, really. But thank you so much. The cake and tea were delightful.'

'Then you must come again. She must, mustn't she Rapha?'

'I'm sure Mademoiselle Honeyman has her own plans for her holiday.' Raphael gave Megan a warm smile.

'Oh, I know!' Lulu suddenly clapped her hands together. 'The benefit evening. We should invite Mademoiselle.'

Megan raised an inquisitive eyebrow.

'We're holding a black tie event here next Friday evening, raising money for a number of charities,' Raphael explained. 'Yes, why don't you come? Bring your sister and her husband, too. What are their names?' He reached for his BlackBerry.

'Thomas and Sarah Cutter.' Megan watched as he tapped it in.

'I'll have an invitation sent over in the next couple of days,' he said.

Megan thought Lulu looked like the cat that had got the cream as she left, but she didn't mind. Who would have thought when she turned up on her sister's doorstep three weeks ago that she'd soon be attending a proper Parisian ball.

Sarah was excited when she told her.

'Oh, I've always wanted to get into one of those society events. Really Meg, Tom and I have been working on it for ages then you turn up and within a couple of weeks you've snapped up an invitation.'

'Being a school teacher does have its rewards.' Megan grinned.

'Thank heavens you're not in an inner city comp,' said her sister. 'You'd never meet anyone there. Now, have you got anything to wear?'

'The dress I wore to the restaurant the other day.'

'Oh, no, this calls for proper dressing up!' Sarah clapped her hands together. 'We're going shopping.'

★ ★ ★

Sarah was definitely out to impress: she bought a dress at Dior. Megan's tastes were more restrained and she settled on a dress from a little boutique in a deep plum silk that skimmed her hips but didn't reveal too much on top. It was cheaper than Sarah's, but still more than she'd wanted to spend.

It was raining when the cab turned up to transport them across the river, a muggy evening following the heat of the day which had been broken by an earlier storm.

'Just our luck,' Sarah complained. 'We'll be soaked in no time.'

Tom, dashing in his dinner suit,

glanced at Megan and shrugged, as if he was used to his wife picking fault. She did seem to be more contentious these days, Megan had noticed.

The nights drew in early in Paris in August and when they arrived at the house light was already spilling out from the open front door like a golden carpet on the slick steps. Megan held an umbrella over her sister as they made a dash for the entrance.

'Wow!' Sarah looked up. 'Now this really is the posh side of town.'

Their invitation was checked by a burly man with an ear-piece and a no-nonsense glower on his face. When he finally waved them through there were staff waiting to take their outdoor things and to direct them up the stairs.

The sound of a band playing, the buzz of conversation and the clink of glasses drifted down to greet them. Waiters made their way unobtrusively through the guests, offering glasses of champagne. Sarah was quick to lift one off a tray and taste it.

'Mmm, the good stuff,' she pronounced. 'Well, Meg, you've certainly got yourself in here.' She led the way into the ballroom.

Megan paused on the threshold and took in the mirrored panels and grand chandeliers. At one end a five piece band played on a raised dais. Some of the guests were dancing. French conversation bubbled from every group. Tonight would test her language as well as her social skills.

She scanned the room for Raphael, eventually locating him in a corner with Maryam d'Aneste hanging off his arm as they greeted guests. The woman looked particularly stunning this evening, skin glowing, diamonds sparkling at her throat, hair swept up. Not only had she bared her arms but most of her back too. That took confidence.

'So that's your Raphael,' Sarah said at her side, following her gaze across the room.

'He's not my Raphael,' Megan protested.

'And that must be his fiancée. Lucky you're not in competition with her.'

'Thank you very much, sis.'

Sarah was right of course; even if she did like Raphael Santerre and he wasn't already engaged, there was no way she would have pitted herself against Maryam d'Aneste.

'Mademoiselle Honeyman.'

Megan turned around to see Lulu pushing through the crowds towards her. Her cream sleeveless gown had a plain bodice and a skirt that flared from her slim hips. The clumpy boots were gone; flat ballet pumps graced her feet.

'Lulu, you look gorgeous!' Megan exclaimed. The girl blushed at the genuine compliment.

'Merci. So do you, Mademoiselle. You don't look like a teacher at all!'

Sarah laughed at her side.

'This must be your sister,' Lulu transferred her attention to Sarah.

'Lulu, my sister and brother-in-law Monsieur and Madame Cutter.'

'Enchanté.' Lulu offered her hand.

'Let me introduce you to Raphael.'

'That would be excellent!' Sarah gushed, spotting an opportunity.

Before Megan could object, her sister set off after Lulu. She and Tom had no option but to follow.

'That's Sarah,' Tom whispered wryly. 'Into social mobility. She'll seize upon any chance.'

'Rapha!' Lulu cried, on reaching her brother. 'Here's Mademoiselle Honeyman. And I want to introduce you to her sister and her husband — Monsieur et Madame Cutter.'

Megan noticed how pointedly Lulu ignored Maryam.

'Please to meet you,' Tom stepped forward, gave a a warm handshake. 'Thank you for the invitation.'

'My pleasure.' Raphael smiled.

'It's a delight to be here,' Sarah added. 'Megan's told us all about you.'

'Sssh!' The warning died on Megan's lips; she felt mortified.

'Really?' Raphael raised an eyebrow.

'I told her how grateful I am for your

103

generosity in arranging that private viewing at Versailles,' Megan explained quickly.

But Sarah's comment had sparked something in the woman at Raphael's side. She turned to Megan, as if seeing her for the first time.

'Lulu's school teacher,' she observed. 'You were at the restaurant the other night. Très charmante.' Her smile never reached her glacial eyes.

'And she's a writer,' Lulu piped up.

'I'm sure she is,' Maryam d'Aneste agreed. She leaned in to Raphael. 'Darling, Monsieur et Madame Brun . . . ' she nodded in the direction of the door. 'You really must greet them.'

'I'll catch up with you later,' Raphael's warm smile included them all. 'Enjoy yourselves. Excuse me.'

Lulu sniffed as Maryam steered her brother away.

'Let's find something to eat,' said Tom.

'I see what you mean,' Sarah slipped her arm through Megan's and led her over to the buffet. 'He's gorgeous. No wonder you've fallen for him.'

'I haven't fallen for him.'

'Come on Meg, you can't kid me.'

'He's engaged.'

'Oh yes, you can tell she's got her claws into him,' Sarah drained her glass of champagne. 'And she's marked you.'

'Really?'

'Classic case. If you didn't see it you must be blind.' Sarah deposited her empty glass on the tray of a passing waiter and picked up a full one.

Megan glanced back across the room to where Raphael was greeting the Bruns. Maryam looked completely at home on his arm.

Maryam d'Aneste had marked her? She very much doubted it; she wasn't even in the same league.

8

Everyone at the Santerre's party seemed either to be wealthy or worthy and as Megan was neither, she felt out of place. It wasn't her sort of thing at all. She didn't know anyone and found that conversation tended to peter out after she told people what she did for a living. The strain of trying to converse in French was also tiring her out.

Tom and Sarah were both gladhanding people, working as a team, so maybe things had settled down between them. Megan nibbled canapés, drank champagne and tried not to stand out like a sore thumb.

Eventually she went out into the hallway and sat down on the stairs. She watched the waiters come and go from the kitchens and the two security men standing chatting out of the corners of their mouths at the door, so that it looked as if they were still paying attention to their jobs.

She gazed up at the glass cupola, blackly opaque under the night sky and wondered what she was doing in a place like this. She would certainly have some tales to tell in the staff room come September.

'I agree. It is noisy in there.'

Megan started. Raphael sat down on the stair at her side, loosening his cravat. Her senses were immediately embraced by that unique scent of coconut and vanilla she'd first encountered at Versailles.

'Where's Maryam?' she asked looking around.

'Speaking to Pierre Duval, the president of a shipping company.'

'And aren't you meant to be schmoozing your guests?'

'They can wait.' He sighed. 'I think you've chosen the best place.'

The two security men down below, suddenly aware that the boss had appeared, abruptly moved apart and stiffened their backs.

'There are too many of these evenings,' Raphael confided.

'Perhaps you want the quieter life in Amboise,' Megan suggested. 'Or if you really want a quiet life, come to Winhampton College. The nearest town is fifteen miles away.'

He looked at her and smiled.

'I probably sound dissatisfied,' Megan smoothed down the skirt of her dress. 'I'm not really. School's not that bad.'

'You look lovely tonight.'

Megan was so shocked that her mouth dropped open.

'Lulu keeps pointing it out,' he said.

Megan closed her mouth. Maybe he wouldn't have noticed himself.

'So, you sometimes get tired of these events,' Megan diverted the conversation back to him.

'Papa put a lot of money through his foundation — he was a great supporter of the arts and good causes. I feel I should continue, for him.'

'Responsibilities.' Megan nodded. She

looked at him keenly. 'Most people seem to think that if you're wealthy you must have this incredible freedom. It's not always true though, is it?'

'I have to fly to New York again in September, then Hong Kong. There are meetings all the time.'

'Ever thought of letting it all go?' Megan said suddenly, then realised how impertinent that must sound. He didn't seem to take offence.

'Frequently,' he admitted frankly. 'Yet I feel I need to honour Papa's memory, especially with his death being so recent.'

'What do you like to paint?' Megan toyed with the carved banister.

'I used to do a lot of family portraits,' he said. 'They're all stacked in a small room at the house in Amboise. Sometimes I painted by the river, but there never was much time for it with studying and work.'

'Where did you study?'

'The Sorbonne, and I spent some time in London — Economics and

International Relations. I wanted to study art, but I knew I would have to take over the family business interests in time so it wasn't appropriate.'

'Too much of life seems to be about what's appropriate.'

'Is that why you're teaching?'

Megan shrugged. 'It was a job and a roof over my head. Actually I quite like it, but it's not what I really want to be doing.'

'How much writing have you done since you've been in Paris?'

'I've started. It's still mostly research. Where do you start with a subject as huge as Louis Quatorze?'

'Have you ever visited Amboise?' he said suddenly.

Megan shook her head.

'You ought to visit the castle. There's a lot of royal history surrounding it.'

'Yes, I know. Maybe I will some day.' It hung in the air between them. 'There are lots of other places too,' she said quickly in case he thought she was angling for an invitation: 'Chenonceau,

Chambord, Vaux le Vicomte — I'll get to see them all eventually.'

Megan looked up as two people came down the stairs pausing to look at Raphael quizzically.

'Perhaps you'd better go back in,' Megan suggested.

'You're right. I can't stay out here all night.' He got up briskly then held out his hand. 'Do you want to dance?'

'Oh, um . . . all right. Why not?'

She allowed him to help her up and followed him back into the ballroom. The band were playing a swing number. Raphael entwined his hand with hers, placed the other on her waist and they moved in time together. Occasionally he would spin her around before bringing her back into contact with him.

Megan didn't feel self conscious at all. She lost herself in the music. Since this was probably the first and only time she would ever be this close to Raphael Santerre, she was going to make the most of it.

As she danced she forgot about Dev, about her parents, forgot about school and her mundane life. Suddenly anything seemed possible. She was young, she had potential, and the whole of her life lay before her.

Lulu was watching them. She looked pleased. For all Megan knew Lulu might have encouraged her brother to ask her to dance. It didn't matter, Megan decided. The music ended.

'That was great!' Megan enthused, laughing with the sheer joy of it. 'You're a good mover.'

'You too,' he returned the compliment, grinning with pleasure.

'Raphael.' The mutual appreciation was broken by the appearance of Maryam d'Aneste. She touched her fiance's arm, spoke in rapid French.

'Excuse me,' Raphael smiled at Megan before disappearing into the crowds, but not before Maryam d'Aneste had thrown her a look which made her feel like she was a nobody.

Megan wandered back to the buffet;

she was suddenly ravenous.

'So,' Sarah sidled up to her. 'What was that about?'

'What?' Megan frowned.

'You and Raphael Santerre. I'd say there was chemistry there.'

'Don't be daft. We just both like dancing.'

'Oh I think it's more than that,' Sarah chuckled slyly. 'For him, too.'

Megan stared at her sister incredulously.

'Pity he's spoken for. You might have had a chance otherwise. Imagine, all that money, this house . . . ' She gazed around appraisingly.

Megan clicked her tongue impatiently and turned away; sometimes her sister's materialism annoyed her. Nevertheless, as she nibbled on some crudités, her gaze sought out Raphael across the room. He stood tall and elegant in his black suit, the pristine white cuffs and collar contrasting with his olive skin, his hair, a little longer than fashion dictated, stylishly layered.

She noted his intense concentration as he listened to conversation, as if nothing mattered more than the person he was with. He must be like that with everyone, so obviously the dance and even their talk beforehand had meant nothing; he was merely being polite to his sister's school teacher. And yet . . .

After a while, realising what she was doing, Megan turned away.

'Do you wanna dance?'

Megan looked up to see Tom.

'Where's Sarah?'

'Oh she's found someone she knows from the gallery, someone who's spent a lot of money there recently.' He spoke as if he didn't care.

Dancing with Tom took her mind off Raphael and was a lot of fun. She remembered that before he became a serious trader working all hours, Tom Cutter had been a crazy guy into watersports and partying.

* * *

A little later, Megan was washing her hands in the sumptuous marble, verbena-scented bathroom when the door opened and Maryam d'Aneste appeared. The woman came in, leant over the sink next to Megan to examine her face in the mirror, brushing a mascaraed eyelash that had dared to break formation.

'So you're Lulu's teacher,' she said as Megan replaced the thick, fluffy towel. She leaned back against the marble washbasin surround, and looked Megan up and down. 'You know of course that Raphael and I are getting married.'

'Yes, I know.'

'We've known each other since we were children. We both come from wealthy families; we move in the same world. And you're a teacher. How nice. This must be your summer holiday.'

'I'm staying with my sister. Her husband works in finance. They live in the Marais,' Megan felt the need to hit back.

'And when are you leaving?'

'Not until the end of the month. Raphael wanted me to talk to Lulu, to find out why she doesn't want to return to school.'

The cool blonde continued to observe her as if she were not only from another caste but another planet.

'Ah, yes, Lulu,' Maryam smiled. 'Tiresome child. Gets ridiculous notions into her head at times.'

'She's a teenager who's recently been orphaned,' Megan pointed out.

'Boarding school is the best place for her. I expect you're looking forward to getting back there yourself. Do you have anyone? A boyfriend?'

'Not at the present time.'

'Well, I'm sure you'll find someone one day,' Maryam turned back to the mirror, widened her eyes again. 'One word of advice . . . '

Megan met her gaze through the mirror.

'Don't let Lulu put any ideas into your head, especially about her brother. She's very good at doing that. Quite the manipulator really.'

There was nothing more to say. Not for one moment did Megan believe that Maryam had actually come to touch up her make-up. She'd deliberately followed Megan to warn her off.

The evening had lost its appeal. She sought out Sarah in the ballroom.

'I'm getting tired now.' Megan stifled a yawn. 'How are you doing?'

'I think I'd better get Tom away from the free bar,' Sarah glowered.

Megan followed her gaze across the room to see her brother-in-law, glass in hand, chatting up a svelte woman with long legs.

'I'll meet you downstairs,' Megan said, but Lulu waylaid her before she was halfway to the door.

'Oh, Mademoiselle Honeyman!' the youngster gushed. 'I've had a brilliant idea. Let's tell my brother.'

'I'm leaving now, Lulu.'

'This won't take a moment.'

She tugged Megan's arm and Megan had no choice but to allow herself to be led across the room to Raphael. Maryam d'Aneste, at his side, did not look at all pleased to see Megan coming in their direction, especially not in the company of Lulu.

'Rapha!' Lulu called out.

He glanced up from his conversation with Maryam.

'Cheri,' he greeted his sister.

'I've had an idea. Tell me what you think of it.'

Megan shrugged helplessly to indicate she was as much in the dark as him. Raphael smiled at her.

'I don't have to go back to school,' Lulu declared.

'Lulu, we've talked about this . . . '

'I have the perfect solution. I can be home schooled. You can hire Mademoiselle Honeyman to be my tutor!'

9

Stunned by Lulu's unexpected proposition, Megan didn't know where to put herself. Maryam d'Aneste glowered at her. Lulu looked triumphant. As for Raphael, she couldn't work out from the expression on his face what he thought about the suggestion. Eventually Megan found her voice.

'That's a wild idea, Lulu. It would be nice to have been consulted on it first but, of course, it's impossible.' Then she smiled at Raphael. 'Thank you for a wonderful evening. We're leaving now.' And she shook his hand firmly and walked out.

'What was all that about?' Sarah asked wide-eyed as they waited in the hallway for a cab.

'I have no idea. It was nothing to do with me.' Of course she knew what it was about.

'Good idea though,' Sarah slipped into her coat as Tom held it. 'That would keep you close to dreamy Raphael. You should consider it.'

'Oh, should I?' Megan snapped. 'I do have a life, you know and I resent a fourteen-year-old girl trying to use me for her own ends!'

'I mean, who do they think I am?' She was still fuming at being patronised and warned off by Maryam d'Aneste. This was supposed to be a holiday and she'd been dragged into something that was none of her doing. Why couldn't she just get back to Louis XIV and forget about the whole lot of them?

She kept quiet during the drive back to the apartment, watching the lights of the city speed past the rain-streaked windows.

Sarah, however, was more animated than she'd seen her for a while.

'Did you speak with Monsieur Desamme?' she asked her husband. 'He's the Chairman of Desamme Futures; he could do a lot for your career. I slipped him your number. We mustn't waste opportunities. René Malvoisier was telling me about an apartment that might become available in Les Invalides at the end of August. I think we should see it.'

'That's an expensive area,' Tom pointed out.

'We should be moving up, Tom.'

He didn't reply.

'You ought to tell her,' Megan said once they were back at the apartment while Sarah was out of the room. 'She's busy making plans for you to spend more money and you might not have a job. She deserves to know.'

'And I will, when the time is right,' he ran a hand through his hair. 'Please let me do it in my own time.'

'Of course. I won't say anything.'

'Thanks,' he slipped an arm about her shoulders and kissed the top of her head. 'Anyway, thanks for a great evening.'

Megan called goodnight to Sarah then climbed the stairs. As she undressed for her shower, she could still discern a hint of coconut and vanilla on her dress where she and Raphael had danced close together. She laid it out over the back of a chair. It would have to be dry-cleaned, but perhaps not straight away.

As she came out of the shower she could hear raised voices coming from downstairs. Poor Tom, Megan thought. Sarah had always been demanding. Tom was going to have to tell her soon and who knew what would happen when he did. It looked as if she might have to pick up the pieces. Megan sighed; going back to school was going to be restful compared to this holiday.

The following morning Megan set out into the city once more, determined to put the previous evening behind her. Her mobile rang as she walked along a busy street. It was Mike Havers.

'Mike!' she exclaimed, surprised.

'Obviously not who you were expecting,' he quipped at the other end. 'How's the holiday going?'

'It's fine, great. I'm getting a lot of research done.'

'Remember I said I'd ring?'

'Yes you did. Where are you?' She stepped around a mother remonstrating with a pouting child on the pavement. A group of Japanese tourists rushed by.

'I'm at St Pancras, about to board the Eurostar. I'm coming to Paris for a few days. I've booked a hotel. How about dinner tonight?'

There was no reasonable excuse she could give not to. Besides it might be nice to get in touch with the reality of school and her other life after the wild couple of weeks she'd had. He gave her the name of the hotel where he was staying and she said she'd come to him.

'About eight?' he suggested.

Sarah seemed pleased when Megan told her she was meeting up with the science master from school.

'Probably more in your league,' she reflected, causing Megan to bristle. 'Why don't you bring him to dinner tomorrow? I'll tell Madame Boursin.'

Megan wasn't sure whether she wanted to commit to another evening with Mike until she was certain how tonight would go, yet it would be churlish to refuse now he was in Paris.

'You and Tom were arguing last night,' she shifted the focus away from herself. 'I thought you'd had a good evening.'

'Yes, well, sometimes Tom isn't as committed as he should be,' Sarah waved a dismissive hand.

'Perhaps he has a lot on his mind,' Megan said tentatively. 'He's a good man Sarah. Don't take him for granted. Talk to him.'

'He'll just want to talk about babies and I'm afraid that discussion is closed,' her sister said sharply and walked out of the room.

★ ★ ★

Megan took the Metro to the hotel. It wasn't quite up to the standard of some of the venues she'd been frequenting lately.

Mike was waiting for her in reception. His face lit up as she walked in.

'Bonjour!' He grinned.

He was dressed casually in chinos and an open-necked shirt, his brown hair cropped close to his head. He looked sensible and reliable and, if she was honest, a bit boring. But then she was being unfair.

He led her into a restaurant full of families and tourists.

'So what have you been up to in Paris?' he said enthusiastically as they studied the menu.

'I've been researching palaces and churches and town houses. I've seen most of what I've wanted to see. And, do you know Lulu Santerre?'

'The French girl in Year Nine?'

'Gill asked me to get in touch with her family. She doesn't want to come back to school in the autumn. Gill thought I might be able to get to the bottom of it.'

'And?'

'It's complicated.'

'She's a fine student.' Mike looked up as the waiter arrived. 'Steak, medium rare, please' he ordered, handing back the large menu.'

Megan opted for grilled fish.

'Bit rich having to deal with school business on holiday,' Mike grinned.

'It's had its compensations.' Megan shrugged. 'Her guardian took me out to a posh restaurant the other evening, and last night we went to a ball at the family mansion.'

'Quite right, too,' Mike said generously. 'Is she coming back?'

'I really don't know,' Megan sighed. 'It depends on what her brother decides to do with his life, but it's really no concern of mine. Let's not talk about school. What are your plans for the summer?'

'I thought I'd take the TGV down south.' He topped up his wine glass. 'I fancy seeing what Cannes is like, maybe visit Monaco.'

Megan laughed. 'You don't strike me as the type to go gambling or mixing with the celebs on the Cote d'Azur.'

'Not all scientists are geeks.'

'I guess I shouldn't label people.'

The meal arrived and although Megan had said she didn't want to talk about school it was the one thing they had in common and so conversation kept straying back there: who was sounding fed-up with life, whether Edina Swank would get promoted to house mistress, exam results, who would land the contract for re-roofing the gym and wouldn't it have been better to have got it done over the summer holiday?

It was a safe, comfortable world, but the more they talked the more Megan questioned whether she really wanted to belong to it. It was only meant to be a stop-gap and now she was about to enter her third year.

'Do you ever think of doing something else?' she asked, her fork poised over her half-eaten fish.

'Everybody thinks of doing something

127

else,' Mike said. 'But reality kicks in doesn't it? I enjoy teaching and in this uncertain economic climate it's good to have a secure job. The pay's good, so are the long holidays. You could do worse.'

She grimaced.

'Anyway, don't you relish the challenge of shaping youngsters' minds?'

'We don't get to do a lot of that these days.' Megan privately thought no-one would be able to shape Lulu Santerre's mind.

'You're an old cynic, Megan Honeyman, and in a romantic city like Paris, too.' He shook his head. 'So, what are you doing tomorrow?'

She hadn't given it much thought.

'Why don't you show me around?' he suggested.

It seemed like a good idea. It would certainly take her mind off Lulu Santerre and her brother.

'My sister's invited you to dinner, by the way,' she said.

'She's married to an American isn't she?'

'You remembered.'

'Don't sound so surprised; I remember a lot of the things you tell me.'

It felt strange sitting in a restaurant in Paris with someone from school. Megan felt as if she'd entered another world over the past few weeks, and it was hard to be pulled back.

Mike was the perfect gentleman. Even when she said it was time to leave, he insisted on calling her a cab and paying for it. He kissed her briefly on the cheek as she waited for it to pull up in the street.

'I'll meet you at the foot of the Eiffel Tower at eleven,' he said.

There was no getting out of it, she was committed to spending time with Mike Havers. Perhaps it would do her good.

★ ★ ★

As always, the Eiffel Tower was packed with tourists and street sellers, a myriad of languages and clicking cameras.

129

Somehow she found Mike in the middle of the heaving masses.

'Are we going up?' He jerked his head at the iron structure.

'It's a long wait.' Megan looked dubious. 'And I'm not very good with heights. You can get just as good a view of Paris from Montmartre and it doesn't cost anything.'

'Okay, I bow to your greater experience.' He grinned.

'We should start with a river cruise,' Megan advised. 'Follow me.'

Evidently, Mike had never been to Paris before for he relied on her guidance totally. They did all the touristy things — coffee at a pavement café, gardens and palaces, the Champs Elysees, the Arc de Triomphe. There was too long a queue for the Louvre, and in a way she was glad — she didn't want to share Louis and Hyacinthe Rigaud with him; somehow, after Versailles, that seemed connected to Raphael.

At the end of the afternoon they

arrived in Montmartre.

'It's over-commercialised.' Megan nodded at the tacky souvenir shops and the artists in the square.

'Love it!' Mike gushed.

'I didn't take you for the touristy type,' Megan looked at him keenly.

'Then, you need to get to know me better, don't you?' He chuckled.

She didn't reply but quickly moved on. The view from the top of the Sacré Coeur was breathtaking. Once more, Megan felt that she didn't want to leave, that she could belong to this city.

'Are you expecting a call?' Mike said us once again she pulled out her phone and frowned at it. 'You've been looking at it all day.'

'Oh, no,' she put it away. 'It's just . . . There's unfinished business with Lulu Santerre. I'm half expecting her brother to get in touch again.'

'Do you think it would help if I had a chat with her?'

'No!' she said quickly.

'That sounds very definite.'

'I mean, it's difficult enough for the girl to have one teacher pestering her. We don't want to completely ruin her school holidays, do we? Remember when you were her age.'

He grinned at her side.

'Okay. I'll leave the poor girl in peace. I'm sure you can be very persuasive.' He leaned on the wall and looked up at her. 'You could persuade me to do most things.'

'Mike,' she chided, moving away and retracing her steps back down from the church.

'I've had a great day.' He hurried to catch up with her. 'Haven't you?'

She had to admit that she had.

'We get on well.'

Again, that much was true.

'School is a small world. We don't have much chance to get out.'

Was he saying that they should settle for what they could get?'

'Anyway,' he quickly changed the subject, picking up on her lack of enthusiasm, 'are you up for some crepes?'

She laughed. 'Eating is all you've seemed to do today!'

'I'm on holiday. I'll work it off when I get back to school,' he protested good naturedly. 'I'm looking forward to tonight. Is your sister a good cook?'

'Actually she employs someone to cook.'

'I hope she's nothing like Ada Walcott!'

They couldn't help smiling at the thought of the school cook producing dinner in Paris.

10

Tom paused briefly in the act of pouring red wine into Mike's glass.

'So how long have you been at Winhampton, Mike?' he asked.

'Five years.' Mike took an appreciative sip. 'I started off teaching in an inner city comp. After a couple of years I decided I needed to get out into the country and this job came up.'

'Are girls easier than boys?' Sarah asked.

'Don't you believe it!' He laughed. 'They tend to be brighter academically, but they can be bitchy, can't they?' He looked to Megan for confirmation and she nodded.

Mike Havers seemed to have slotted in easily, Megan thought. He'd turned up on time for dinner, brought wine, complimented Sarah on her dress and had got Tom chatting about American football.

'He's nice,' Sarah said when they'd finished the meal and Megan followed her into the kitchen to load the dishwasher and make coffee. Madame Boursin hadn't been asked to stay late, as she would have been if Sarah had been intending to impress a business contact. 'Nice, but a bit . . . ' Sarah searched for the word, 'ordinary, I suppose. Still, it's clear he likes you and — let's face it, Meg — you're not getting any younger.'

'Thanks very much!'

'You know what I mean.' Sarah reached up for the coffee cups. 'Where are you going to meet someone stuck in that school of yours? It's classic if you think about it — two lonely school teachers hooking up.'

'I'm not lonely, and I'm not going to be a school teacher forever. And we're certainly not hooking up!' Megan almost dropped a dish as she thrust it into the dishwasher.

'Careful,' Sarah cautioned. She set the cups out on a tray. 'Oh, so you're not going to be stuck in that school forever. Maybe coming to Paris has done something for you then.' Now she smiled.

'Yesterday, when we were at Sacré Coeur and I looked out over the city, I had the feeling that I might like to stay.' Megan softened too.

'What about taking up the offer?'

'What offer?'

'The one that Santerre girl made as we were leaving the other night?'

'That was no offer. It was Lulu being silly because she thinks she can prise her brother away from his fiancée.' Megan coloured.

'Oh really, so you're supposed to be bait,' Sarah chuckled.

'It's not funny. It's childish. I'm not going to allow myself to be manipulated by a fourteen-year-old pupil.'

'They did make a handsome pair, Raphael Santerre and his fiancée.'

'They move in the same circles,' Megan said, shutting the door of the dishwasher. 'Lulu will just have to grow up.'

'So you really don't see yourself with Mike?' Sarah probed.

How could she say that since meeting Raphael Santerre Mike Havers seemed bland in comparison? Even though she could never have Raphael she knew now that she couldn't just settle for second best, it wouldn't be fair to her — or to Mike.

'You met your Mr Right,' she said. 'Why shouldn't I hold out for mine?'

'It's not all it's cracked up to be.' Sarah fetched the cream and sugar.

'I think the two of you need to talk to each other,' Megan said pointedly.

Before Sarah could reply Tom appeared in the doorway.

'Is the coffee arriving any time tonight?'

Sarah rolled her eyes. 'It's on its way,' she said impatiently.

The rest of the evening was pleasant enough. Mike seemed reluctant to leave but as the clock struck eleven he finally got up.

'Thank you for a wonderful evening,' he said.

'If you were here for longer we'd ask you to come again.' Sarah smiled.

'I'm heading to Cannes in a couple of days. I wouldn't mind some company.' He darted Megan a quick look before reaching for his coat. 'So how about it?'

'What?'

'Come to Cannes with me. We've still got three weeks before the start of term. You can come to the south of France for a week and you'll still have time in Paris at the end. What do you think?'

'Mike.' She sighed.

'You have plans here?'

'I'm researching my book.'

'It's good to take a break sometimes. Look, Megan, we've had a great day, we enjoy each other's company. You're not seeing anyone . . . '

'I can't,' she said. 'I like you as a friend Mike but . . . '

'Enough said.' He smiled sadly. 'Shall we meet up tomorrow?'

She hesitated.

'I want to go to the science park,' he

explained. 'See if I can pick up any ideas for the kids.'

'Strictly school?'

'I'll try,' he grinned.

They both knew the moment had passed.

'Well?' said Sarah when Megan returned to the drawing-room. 'Are you booking a ticket to Cannes?'

Megan shook her head.

'Pity. He seems like a nice guy.'

'I'm going to bed.'

Megan wondered what she'd done as she lay in bed, staring up at the high ceiling. She'd turned down an opportunity for romance and travel and adventure, and for what? An illusion, a dream of something that was never going to happen. But if it wasn't right, it wasn't right. If that meant she had to be alone, so be it . . .

★ ★ ★

If Megan had thought things would be awkward with Mike the following day she was proved wrong. They met at his hotel and took the Metro out to the Parc de la Villette. She had to admit it was refreshing to do something unconnected to Louis XIV.

'See, science is fun,' Mike said as Megan played around with the children's interactive exhibits.

'If only you could bring the girls here,' she said.

'A field trip to Paris — old Bursar Hoskins would have a fit!'

They both laughed.

'I still think we'd be good together,' Mike said suddenly. 'Maybe you won't come to Cannes with me but there's always school.'

'And I will see you there in three weeks' time,' Megan said firmly, closing the door on any more discussion about the rest of the holiday.

He shrugged acceptance and turned his attention back to a robotic display. Megan enjoyed watching him. His enthusiasm was infectious. He was a good guy, she reflected. Her phone rang. Raphael Santerre's voice instantly banished all thoughts of Mike.

'Have I caught you at an inconvenient time?' Raphael asked.

'No. I'm out with a friend from school,' she didn't mention a name. 'Thank you for the other night, by the way.'

'About that; I need to talk to you.' He sounded apologetic. 'Lulu and I had a row. She stayed at a friend's house last night. I need to find out what's going on. Can we meet?'

Megan looked at Mike, who was watching her.

'I'll be free later this afternoon,' she offered.

They arranged to meet at a café near the opera house at four o'clock.

'Who was that?' Mike asked as she snapped her phone shut.

'Lulu Santerre's brother, Raphael. He needs to talk to me about Lulu. I've got to meet him later. Do you mind?'

'You're putting in a lot of work for the school on holiday,' he said.

'So are you with your science exhibits,' she pointed out weakly.

'Oh, I just said that.' He grinned. 'This is really for me, not the girls.'

Megan tried to pay attention to Mike and what they were doing for the rest of the day but it was hard to keep her mind off her meeting with Raphael. Finally, at three o'clock they set off back to the city.

'I guess I'll see you back at school, then,' Mike said as they parted. 'Have a good holiday.' He leaned in and kissed her on the cheek. She could tell he was watching her as she walked away.

★　★　★

The café was busy; she wondered if she'd find a table but Raphael was already waiting for her. He rose from his chair when he saw her.

'Megan, thank you. I'm sorry for disturbing your day.'

'Not at all,' she said, sitting down on the chair he held out for her.

He resumed his seat and signalled for the waiter.

'Just coffee,' Megan told the young man who came to take the order.

All around was the buzz of conversation and the clinking of cups. The smell of roasting coffee and cigarette smoke permeated the air while outside the Paris traffic growled past people relaxing at tables on the pavement. Megan realised how much she loved it all. She turned her attention back to Raphael.

'You're all dressed up for such a hot day,' she commented.

'I've come from the office,' he explained. 'And I have another meeting at five-thirty.'

'So we'd better make this quick,' Megan said as the coffee arrived.

'I do appreciate this; I know it's your holiday.' He looked earnest.

'You keep saying that, and I really don't mind.' She would have forgiven him anything, she realised, glad of the opportunity just to see him again.

'So, Lulu's being stroppy, is she?'

'Stroppy, what is this stroppy?' He looked puzzled.

'It's another word for difficult.'

'Très difficult.' He nodded. 'I'm sorry for what she said as you were leaving the other night. My sister has some bizarre ideas at times.'

Megan shrugged.

'Of course you're not going to leave your career and your home to become a governess to one spoilt teenager. I don't know what's got into her these days.' He shook his head. 'I told her after the party how rude she'd been and how I would no longer tolerate her attitude. She left a note this morning to say she's gone to stay with Mimi Leconte, a friend of hers, tonight. I don't know what's causing this.'

'She's worried about you.' Megan took a cautious sip of her coffee.

'Why?' He frowned.

Megan, feeling mesmerised by his dark eyes, looked away.

'Megan, if you know something, please tell me. If it means breaking a confidence,' he paused, 'please consider what will be best for Lulu.'

When she looked at him again his eyes were pleading.

'She doesn't want you to marry Maryam d'Aneste,' Megan told him. 'Lulu thinks she's not right for you, that she doesn't really love you, that she's only concerned about money and position.'

Raphael sat back in his chair, a look of astonishment on his face.

'That's it?'

'She wants to stay around to . . . to save you, to persuade you not to go ahead with the wedding.'

Raphael pulled a hand over his chin.

'Lulu, Lulu,' he said almost to himself.

'She's still a child really,' Megan said. 'Still missing her father only recently died. Perhaps she's afraid that her brother is going to be taken away from her, too, and by a woman she dislikes. I understand your fiancée and Lulu don't have the easiest of relationships.'

'I have to digest this.' Raphael shook his head.

'Don't be too harsh on her. She's doing it because she loves you.'

'But she can't think I'll change my life because of emotional blackmail!' he protested.

'Young girls can believe anything. She's quite determined.'

A slight smile curled the edges of his mouth. 'That's Lulu.'

Megan concentrated on her coffee as Raphael looked out of the window. She wanted to tell him she agreed with Lulu's assessment of Maryam but it was none of her business.

Finally Raphael turned back to her.

'I must speak to Lulu about this,' he said. 'I have to settle this matter once and for all. Thank you Megan.' He glanced at his watch. 'I have to go.' He pulled out his wallet, set some notes down on the table. 'Stay and enjoy,' he said. Then he was gone.

That was it, so abrupt. She craned her neck to watch him crossing the road and disappearing into a sidestreet. Then with a sigh she inspected the money on the table. There was far more than was needed. She summoned the waiter again, ordered a cream and pastry confection; food seemed the only comfort available now.

She wondered if she'd see Raphael again now that he knew the truth, and whether Lulu would forgive her for betraying a confidence?

* * *

As Megan let herself into the apartment she heard raised voices coming from the drawing-room. Madame Boursin appeared, shrugging on her coat.

'I go. Monsieur tell me to go home this evening,' she said. She looked relieved.

Worried, Megan cautiously entered the drawing-room. Tom stood before the marble fireplace, a pained expression on his face. Her sister was remonstrating with him, arms raised high as she gesticulated.

'Not a word! Not a word!' she was saying. 'How could you do this to me? It's all part of a plan isn't it? You always wanted to go back to that family of yours! You think you can drag me back to Boston!'

'Do you really think I wanted this?'

'Yes, yes I do. This is my life Tom, how could you take it away from me?'

'I can't talk to you when you're like this,' he said. 'We both need to calm down. I'm going for a walk.'

'Don't you dare walk out on me!' Sarah cried.

He did, nonetheless, starting as he saw Megan in the doorway.

'I've been let go,' he said. 'Look after your sister. I'll talk later.'

Then he was gone. The front door slammed.

'Did you hear that? Did you hear it?' Sarah's eyes looked wild. 'He's lost his job. We've lost everything. We can't keep the apartment on my salary. He says we should go back to Boston!' She clenched her fists in frustration.

For a moment Megan thought her sister was about to look for something breakable to throw across the room. Then Sarah seemed to sag. She collapsed onto the sofa and began to sob. Megan sat beside her and folded her into her arms.

'It'll be all right,' she soothed. 'It'll be fine.' She just didn't know how.

11

Eventually Sarah released herself from Megan's arms, got up from the sofa and began to pace.

'What are we going to do? Tom can't lose his job — he can't. I'm not prepared to leave Paris, to leave this apartment. I have a life here!' She looked appealingly at Megan.

Megan didn't know what to say.

'He'll get another job, I know he will,' Sarah fretted. 'I don't care what he says.'

'I hope he will, but it might not happen for a while.'

'Don't say that!'

Megan shrugged.

'You've always been jealous of what I've got!' Sarah suddenly accused her. 'Jealous of Tom, the money, the lifestyle. You'd just love to see me fail.'

'What?' Megan stared at her sister, speechless.

'You've always been holier than thou, the bigger sister. I know you've criticised my choices, felt I've gone after the wrong things while you've always been the worthy one. Mum and Dad thought so, too — don't think I didn't notice that you were always their favourite. They loved you more.'

'Where did you get all that from? That's nonsense.' Megan said.

'I expect you'll be happy now.'

'How can I be happy, Sarah? You've got it all wrong.'

'I'm not leaving,' her sister warned. 'I'm not giving all this up. We've worked too hard for it.' She flounced out of the room.

Megan retreated to the kitchen and made herself a sandwich. She thought it would be best if she stayed there and kept out of Sarah's way. Now where had that diatribe come from? She had no idea her sister felt that way about her. If she was the worthy sister it was only because she'd never been interested in money or the high life. As long as she had enough to get by she'd never cared. She wasn't into fashion, or designer labels, never read glossy magazines and wouldn't have recognised many celebrities if she'd fallen over them.

She remembered when she'd told Sarah about her plans to go travelling with Dev her sister had been concerned about what sort of job she was going to return to, how long her savings were going to last, and how she thought she was ever going to get a foot on the housing ladder. To Megan the prospect of a life-changing experience had been the important thing, whereas Sarah needed the security of material comforts.

But Megan had never questioned her sister's choices or been jealous of them; it was her life. So where was all this coming from now?

After a while she heard the front door opening and then Tom appeared in the kitchen.

'Had to clear my head,' he explained.

'It's all right,' Megan assured him.

'So it's finally happened?'

'These are difficult times for everyone.' Tom opened the fridge, absentmindedly looked around the shelves, then changed his mind and closed it again. 'I knew she'd go ballistic.'

'Any chance you'll find something else?'

Tom ran a hand through his hair and sighed. 'I don't know,' he answered honestly. 'Ah, well, I'd better go and face the music.'

* * *

There was still tension in the air the following morning.

Tom left early for work; Sarah strolled into the kitchen looking as if she'd barely slept.

'Not going to work today?' Megan queried.

'I don't have to be there until eleven thirty.' Sarah reached for a packet of chocolate croissants and tore it open with purpose.

'I recognise that,' Megan nodded. 'Comfort eating.'

'Wouldn't you, if you'd just had a major bombshell?' Sarah carped.

'I frequently have,' Megan admitted with a rueful grin at her sister.

'What are you up to today, then?' Sarah asked. She poured out some coffee, drew up a stool to the island and began to attack the first of the croissants.

'I don't know.' Megan proceeded to tell her sister about the phone call from Raphael and their meeting in the café.

'I had to tell him what Lulu had told me, the man was beside himself,' she ended. She still felt guilty about betraying Lulu's confidence.

'He seems very keen to keep in touch with you,' Sarah observed.

'I don't know.' Megan sighed. 'One thing all this has shown me — you were right — maybe I should do something more exciting with my life. I'm not sure if I want to go back to school.'

Sarah's head jerked up.

'Maybe I'll stay in Paris.'

'What's the point?' her sister said dejectedly. 'Look where ambition and working hard gets you.'

'Don't say that.' Megan slid off her stool and wrapped her arms about Sarah, instinctively feeling that her sister needed a hug.

'It's all falling apart.' Sarah's voice shook. 'Ever since I lost the baby. Then Mum and Dad died, I've just been waiting for the next disaster to happen.'

'Maybe we should talk about the accident,' Megan said. 'We never have, have we? I'm just as scared as you, Sarah, wondering where the next blow will come from. At least you've always had Tom to talk to. When Dev left me I felt I was alone.'

'I'm sorry, I didn't realise,' Sarah's features softened. 'You'd better have one of these, too.' She pushed the packet of croissants towards Megan.

They talked about that dreadful day three years ago. Megan had got the message about the crash first and had

had to 'phone her younger sister to tell her.

'I resented that, you knowing first,' Sarah said. 'You always knew things first.'

'You were the one who got married first. I was jealous that you had Tom,' Megan confessed.

They talked about Sarah locking away her pain and grief, unable to deal with it, especially in the wake of losing her baby.

'Do you think the ambition, the corporate wife, career-woman stuff is linked to that?' Megan suggested tentatively.

'Things can't let you down, things don't die.' Sarah reached for another croissant.

'I think I did judge you, Sarah. I thought you should have confronted the pain. I wanted some support, too, I wanted to talk to you about Mum and Dad but you shut me out. I couldn't accept that we were different, that we dealt with things in our own way.'

'Do you ever think about them?' Sarah traced a pattern on the counter with a finger.

'Every day.'

'Me, too.'

For the first time in three years they reminisced about their parents. Megan began to feel that she and her sister weren't so different after all.

'We should do this more often,' she sighed as the last recollection petered out along with the last of the croissants. 'Perhaps look at some photos. The end was horrible but we had all those good years to celebrate.'

Sarah scrunched up the empty packet.

'Yes, you're right,' she crossed to the bin and tossed it in. 'Our memories keep them alive.'

She turned round suddenly to face Megan again. 'I don't want to lose Tom.' Her eyes were fearful.

'You're not going to lose him.'

'I couldn't bear it. He's a good guy.'

'I know. You two are good together.'

Megan thought her sister was going to say more. Instead she glanced at the clock above the fridge.

'I'd better get ready for work,' she said.

* * *

Megan was thinking about what she was going to do with her day when the phone rang. It was Raphael and he sounded worried.

'Megan, have you seen Lulu?'

'No, why?'

'She didn't stay with Mimi last night. I phoned to see how she was this morning. And they hadn't seen her at all yesterday.'

'Do you have any idea where she might have gone?'

'I thought she might have come to you.'

'I haven't seen her. What will you do?'

'I've got some contacts in the gendarmerie. I'm going to look for her.'

'Paris is a big place.'

'I can't sit here and do nothing.'

Megan heard a protesting female voice in the background.

'I hope you find her,' she said. 'Will you let me know?'

Megan realised she couldn't sit around waiting and wondering either.

'Sarah!' she called.

Her sister appeared at the top of the stairs.

'Raphael just phoned. Lulu's missing. I'm going out to look for her.'

'Where?' Sarah frowned.

'Your guess is as good as mine. I might be late for dinner.'

She caught up her bag and left the house. Where would a fourteen-year-old girl go? She tried the shops — most girls liked shopping — but Paris was so huge and there were so many people it was like looking for a needle in a haystack.

Perhaps she'd found a sheltered spot in a park. Megan consulted her guide book and set off to cover as many central parks as she could. Churches she discounted — she didn't think Lulu was particularly religious. On every Metro journey she searched the faces on the trains and the platforms or coming towards her on the escalators. On every street she pounded she was constantly scanning, but none of the faces was Lulu's. By the end of the afternoon she was weary and disheartened. Then the phone rang.

'Raphael?' It had to be him.

'I haven't found her yet,' he said.

'Nor me. I'm looking, too.' She told him all the places she'd looked.

'I've been to all Lulu's favourite haunts.' He sounded tired. 'She could even be on her way to Amboise. I've asked Guillaume, the estate manager to look out for her.' He sighed. 'Thank you for looking, Megan. I didn't expect that.'

'I feel I'm involved now,' she said.

'There's a few more places I can try,' he said. 'I'll ring you again later.'

Megan looked around. She was on

the right bank of the Seine. Boats glided by below her, traffic flashed through the trees on the other side of the river. She saw the Musée d'Orsay, remembered the day Lulu had shown her around. Perhaps she was there, losing herself in the Impressionists, trying to make sense of her own world. With fresh impetus Megan set off for the bridge.

Because it was the end of the day there were no queues. Once inside Megan headed for the gallery where she and Lulu had had their conversation a couple of weeks ago. She paused in front of Monet's *Blue Water Lilies,* recalling that when Lulu had said she didn't want her brother to marry Maryam d'Aneste it had actually been all about him, not her. Lulu was worried about him becoming some-thing he wasn't, knowing that her brother's heart was really at Amboise, that he wished he could paint and deal in wine. It wasn't about a fourteen-year-old girl being petulant — she

161

actually had some insight into what would make her brother happy.

But running away would only increase his worries, not lessen them.

There was no sign of Lulu at the museum. Megan realised then the futility of running around Paris aimlessly trying to find one person. But faced with the prospect of going back to the apartment and waiting for Raphael to phone she decided to go in the opposite direction instead. Half an hour later she found herself in front of the Santerre's town house.

Taking a deep breath, she rang the doorbell.

'Hi, I'm Megan, Lulu's teacher,' she said to the butler, in case he'd forgotten. 'I've been looking for Lulu.'

'Ah, come in, please,' the butler had lost his haughtiness. He looked relieved. 'Mademoiselle Lulu has just returned.'

Megan followed him into the drawing room where Lulu was unravelling a scarf from around her neck. She looked none the worse for her escapade. She turned around as Megan entered.

'Mademoiselle!' she said, surprised. 'What are you doing here?'

Megan couldn't help herself; she hurried across the room and clasped Lulu to her in a hug.

'Where have you been? Your brother's been so worried about you. I've spent the day searching the city, and he's still out there looking!' A rush of anger overtook her and Megan had to swallow it down. She released Lulu and stepped back.

'We had a row,' Lulu said nonchalantly. 'Rapha is so stupid sometimes. I didn't know what else to do. Then I realised he'd be worried so I came back.'

'Does he know you're here?' Megan demanded.

'I rang him. He's on his way back.'

'That was a very selfish thing you did!'

Megan turned at the sound of the familiar voice. Maryam d'Aneste came into the room.

163

'If you were a child I'd smack you.'
Lulu pulled a couldn't-care-less face.
'How dare you worry your brother so!'

'I bet you didn't care,' Lulu accused the beautiful blonde.

'I have to care because you're his sister,' came the icy reply. 'But I can't abide children who only consider themselves. I know what you're up to, Lulu, and it's not going to work. And as soon as Raphael and I are married I'm going to make sure you stay in that boarding school and as far away from us as you can possibly get. You have to grow up. And as for you,' she looked directly at Megan. 'You haven't helped.'

'I'm sorry?'

'Giving her ideas.'

'I've done nothing of the sort.' Megan stood her ground. 'It was Raphael who called me in to talk to Lulu. I'm just here on holiday. So please, don't drag me into this. Anyway, Lulu's only concerned about her brother.'

'I don't think it's any of your

business, do you?' Maryam crossed her arms as she regarded Megan disdainfully. 'I think it's time you left this family alone. You take care of your school concerns. I will take care of Raphael.'

'Lulu!'

They all turned at the same time to see Raphael in the doorway.

'Rapha!'

Brother and sister rushed towards each other and hugged. A torrent of French passed between them, a mixture of chiding, apologies and expressions of love. Raphael looked up over Lulu's shoulder, and offered Megan a smile of relief.

'You're not going to punish her?' Maryam demanded in disbelief.

'She's my little sister, my Lulu.'

Raphael's fiancée threw up her hands in despair and stalked out of the room. Megan smiled to herself; she guessed that when it came to a choice between Maryam and Lulu, Lulu was always going to win.

'You went looking for her,' Raphael said in awe.

'She's one of my pupils.' Megan shrugged. 'I have a pastoral responsibility.'

'See, Rapha, at least Mademoiselle Honeyman cares about me,' Lulu said triumphantly.

Raphael smiled.

12

Returning to the apartment as darkness was falling, Megan was barely in the door before Sarah accosted her.

'Well, did you find her? You might at least have told me where you were,' she said.

'Yes, everything's fine,' Megan assured her. 'Lulu went back home. She just needed to clear her head.'

'What a thoughtless child.'

Megan couldn't think of Lulu Santerre in that way now she'd got to know her. Almost to her surprise, she'd discovered she really cared about her.

'I think she's desperately worried about her brother,' she said. 'Anyway, I've left them all in the house together. Maryam was there.'

'Oh,' said Sarah. 'Well, there's dinner in the oven if you want some.'

Left alone, Megan thought again

what a pity it was that the closeness she'd experienced with Raphael and Lulu in those moments after he'd discovered his sister was safe and well had had to end, but Maryam was in the house and Raphael had to get back to her.

'Don't worry,' Megan had said, with understanding. 'I need to get back anyway. My sister's having a crisis. Her husband's just heard he's lost his job so she needs a lot of support at the moment. She doesn't want to leave Paris but it looks as if they might have to if Tom doesn't find something else here straightaway.'

She extracted her plate from the oven now — Sarah had already set a place for her on the island. Megan poured some wine from an opened bottle and reflected on the day as she began to eat. She recalled that sense of panic and concern she'd felt when she'd first heard the news, as if Lulu had been a part of her own family. And she wondered what Raphael would make of the antagonism expressed by his fiancée towards his sister. If Maryam had been able to hide it from him until now, Raphael walking in on them had exposed how she truly felt about Lulu.

Well, as Maryam said, it was really none of her business. She tried and failed to shake off that lingering sense of longing . . . When she'd seen Raphael's delight at finding his sister safe, she, too, had wanted to throw herself into his arms and hug him close. Some women just didn't realise how lucky they were. Or maybe Maryam d'Aneste did and that's why she was hanging on for dear life.

Megan looked up as Tom came into the kitchen.

'Sarah told me about Lulu,' he said.

'Everything's fine,' Megan smiled.

Tom poured himself some wine then sat at her side.

'How are you, Tom?' She sensed he needed to talk.

'Scared that I can't give Sarah what she wants,' he confided. 'I love her, I don't want to lose her.'

'She said the same to me about you.'

'She thinks I want to go back to Boston. It's not that. I just need to know there's a possibility of a family in our future,' he contemplated his wine glass. 'Just because she lost one baby doesn't mean it'll happen again.'

Megan placed a reassuring hand on his.

'Give it time. It's all linked with mum and dad dying. She'll come round.'

He looked at her with gratitude in his eyes.

'Tell her what you've just told me about Boston,' Megan advised him. 'It might help.'

Tom finished his wine, thanked her with a kiss on the cheek and left the kitchen. Megan sighed; these days her life seemed to consist of troubleshooting other people's problems.

★　★　★

A couple of days had passed since Lulu had returned home and she'd heard nothing from the Santerres. Mike had gone to Cannes, and the start of a new term was looming on the horizon. It was definitely time to get back to her research.

She took the train to Vaux le Vicomte, the extravagant palace built by Nicholas Fouquet, superintendent of the king's finances, which Louis sequestered after Fouquet's fall from grace. It was time to forget about Raphael Santerre and concentrate on the reason she'd come to Paris.

Megan soaked up the atmosphere of the place, making plenty of notes. Already an idea was forming about how to map out the first few chapters of her novel.

At first she'd anticipated placing a fictional character at Louis' court. Yet why not write about the Sun King himself? Her stay in Paris had given her such a sense of her subject that she began to feel that such a challenge might be feasible. Although it would take more research and a lot more work.

Megan sat on a bench listening to the soothing splash of a fountain. Perhaps it really was time for a change, time to step out and try something new. She still had her travel funds put by from her aborted world tour with Dev. If she was resigned from school it would mean losing touch with Raphael Santerre because she would no longer be around Lulu, but this was about her life, about striking out alone to do something she really wanted to do.

By the time she got back to Paris she'd come to a decision. But before she could say anything Sarah had some news of her own. Tom was home early, which seemed strange, and he looked cheerful, the constant worry frown of the past couple of weeks completely erased.

'Megan, guess what?' Sarah bounded up from her chair. 'Tom's been offered another job. The money's better and we can stay in Paris.'

'That's great. It's sudden.'

'Your friend, Raphael Santerre.' Tom

grinned. 'He got my number at work. I met with one of his people this afternoon. They offered me a job. It gives me more responsibility and independence. Hell, it was a good deal, I couldn't say no.'

'We don't have to leave!' Sarah gushed.

Megan was astonished that Raphael had remembered, much less acted upon her comment the other evening.

Sarah moved to wrap her arms around Tom.

'We've talked,' she said. 'I've agreed that we'll try for a baby.'

'I knew you two would work it out.' Megan grinned. 'I'm so happy for you both.'

'That Raphael Santerre is quite a friend to have.' Sarah smiled.

Megan was longing to phone to thank him. But first she told Sarah and Tom about her decision.

'I'm going back to school to work out my notice,' she said. 'Then I'm coming back to Paris to continue my research.

I'll get a part time job somewhere, improve my French.'

'You can stay with us,' Sarah offered. 'We need to spend more time together anyway. I know that now. Let's celebrate. Tom, get the champagne out.'

So it was a while before Megan found the opportunity to ring Raphael. For some reason she felt awkward as she spoke.

'I want to thank you for Tom's job,' she said.

'He got it on merit,' Raphael replied. 'I just gave him the opportunity. After all you've done for me it was the least I could do.'

'Thank you anyway. Is Lulu coming back to school?'

'I don't actually know yet. I'm still working on it. She likes you so I might be successful.'

'Actually, I've made a decision myself,' Megan said. 'I'm only going back to work out my notice, then I'm coming back to Paris to concentrate on my book.'

'I'm very pleased for you,' he sounded surprised.

'I'd better go. Tom and Sarah are still celebrating and I really ought to join them.'

'Thank you again Megan. I'm glad to have met you. I have to go — I'm going out of town for a few days and I need to go for my flight.'

'Good luck with the wedding.'

And that was that. She probably wouldn't see him again before she left. Unless Lulu threw another wobbler. She clicked the phone shut and smiled to herself; she wouldn't put it past her.

★ ★ ★

Megan telephoned Gillian Tate as a courtesy before she wrote her letter of resignation.

'I'm so sorry,' the headmistress said. 'You'll be missed. Thank you for following up the Santerre girl so willingly. As far as I'm aware she will be returning in September.'

Now that her time was her own, Megan threw herself into her last couple of weeks in Paris.

She was surprised to get a call from Lulu one day.

'Hello, stranger,' Megan said. 'Are you ready for the new term?'

'That depends,' came the cryptic reply.

'On what?'

'Mademoiselle Honeyman, I haven't had a chance to thank you for being so concerned for me,' Lulu said politely. 'I know you love Versailles. Will you meet me there tomorrow?'

'Yes, of course. I was intending to go back one more time before the end of the holiday.'

'Meet me in the Hall of Mirrors at midday,' said Lulu.

It would be busy then, the crowds of tourists at their height, but not wanting to discourage Lulu, Megan agreed.

★　★　★

The Versailles crowds never seemed to relent Megan observed wryly as she arrived at the palace the following day. She smiled to herself as she recalled that special occasion when Raphael had arranged a private viewing for her; something she would never forget, a memory to cherish.

She queued up now, paid her entrance fee, and pushed her way through milling tourists towards the Hall of Mirrors. Megan knew however many times she came to this place she would never tire of it. For a moment she forgot she was meeting Lulu, caught up as she was in the smell and sounds and atmosphere of the glorious mirrored room. In a strange way the crowds made the past seem more real — though it would have been filled with courtiers rather than tourists, buzzing with activity and gossip all those centuries ago.

Suddenly she saw Lulu waving, pushing her way towards her against the flow of humanity. She wasn't alone, her hand in her brother's as she pulled him along behind her. He looked as surprised to see Megan as she was to see him.

'Good,' Lulu looked satisfied as they drew up.

'You didn't say your brother was coming,' Megan chided.

'Believe me, I had no idea you would be here,' Raphael said. 'Lulu told me she wanted a treat before returning to school, that we should spend some time together and she chose here.'

'You have to tell her,' Lulu beamed at her brother before turning back to Megan. 'Maryam has gone. There will be no wedding.'

'Really?' As Megan looked at Raphael her heart was thumping.

'I'll leave you two alone.' Lulu grinned. 'I'll be out by the fountain. Take as long as you like.' She skipped away before either Megan or Raphael could object. The two of them stood facing each other, alone in a sea of tourists.

'I'm sorry I haven't been in touch,' he spoke first.

'You told me you were going away for a few days.'

'Yes. I've been busy. Ending it with Maryam, of course.' He smiled, sheepishly. 'Lulu was right all along; she wasn't the right woman for me. I'd fallen into the relationship after Papa's death because I knew Maryam, because she was there for me, because it was safe. But Lulu helped me to realise that we wanted different things.'

As he spoke, he kept his eyes on Megan. She felt entranced by his gaze, hardly daring to breathe.

'Anyway I've been tying up loose ends. I'm handing over the day to day running of the business to others. I'm going back to Amboise.'

'To deal in wine?' Megan smiled.

He nodded. 'I might even paint.' He paused. 'You might like to spend some time there, too.'

She didn't immediately respond, lost for words at the turn of events.

'When you told me you were going to leave school and come back to Paris I felt happy.' Raphael continued in a rush. 'It took Lulu to point out the obvious. Megan. I liked you that first day you walked into me here. I thought I'd never see you again. But then fate brought us together again through Lulu. All those meetings, those phone calls, I just wanted to see you again. I began to understand then it was never going to work with Maryam because I'd fallen in love with someone else.' He stopped. 'Say something,' he pleaded.

'By someone else you mean . . . ?' She smiled, deliberately obtuse.

'Yes, you.'

'I just wanted to hear you say it.'

'How do you feel about me?' Raphael Santerre suddenly looked unsure of himself, as if a word could break him.

'The same,' she said gently.

'So I can expect you at Amboise?'

'I might be able to squeeze it in.'

He drew her towards him and kissed her. As she lost herself in the coconut and vanilla embrace Megan thought of all the lovers who had met and stolen kisses in this magnificent place. No book she wrote would ever match up to this.

When they drew apart she glanced out of the window. Down below on the terrace, Lulu stood gazing up, grinning.

Megan smiled; how grateful she was that Lulu Santerre had chanced to disrupt her summer holiday.

THE END

Other titles in the
Linford Romance Library:

EARL GRESHAM'S BRIDE

Angela Drake

When heiress Kate Roscoe compromises herself through an innocent mistake, widower, Earl Gresham steps in with an offer of marriage to save her reputation. She is soon deeply in love with him, but is beset by the problems of overseeing his grand household. The housekeeper is dishonest and the nanny of the earl's two children is heartless and lazy. But a far greater threat comes from his former mistress who will go to any lengths to destroy Kate's marriage.

FINDING ANNABEL

Paula Williams

Annabel had disappeared after going to meet the woman who, she'd just discovered, was her natural mother . . . However, when her sister Jo travels to Somerset to try and find her, she must follow a trail of lies and deceit. The events of the past and the present have become dangerously entangled. And she discovers, to her cost, that for some people in the tiny village of Neston Parva, old loyalties remain fierce and strangers are not welcome . . .

IT WAS ALWAYS YOU

Miranda Barnes

Anna Fenwick is very fond of Matthew, a hard-working young man from her Northumberland village. She has known him all her life, although, sadly, it seems that he is not interested in her. Then Anna embarks on a whirlwind romance with Don, a visiting Canadian and goes to Calgary with him. Life is wonderful for a time. However, her heart is still in Northumberland — but when she returns to seek Matthew, will she eventually find him?

IN HER SHOES

Anne Holman

Inspect Mallison was reluctant to arrest murdered man's son, althou the incriminating evidence was o elming: he'd been alone with ther immediately prior to the r and there'd been a bitter qua Goldstein was killed trying to his will — unfavourably for hi , the weapon, a desk paper-w bore the son's fingerprints, a his father had withdrawn financial support for a new West End play in which his son was to star. Yet still Mallinson wasn't convinced . . .